MADLY IN LOVE

SARAS AZAD

AF517522

Srishti
PUBLISHERS & DISTRIBUTORS

Srishti Publishers & Distributors
A unit of AJR Publishing LLP
212A, Peacock Lane
Shahpur Jat, New Delhi - 110 049

editorial@srishtipublishers.com

First published by
Srishti Publishers & Distributors in 2023

Copyright © Saras Azad, 2023

10 9 8 7 6 5 4 3 2 1

This is a work of fiction. The characters, places, organisations and events described in this book are either a work of the author's imagination or have been used fictitiously. Any resemblance to people, living or dead, places, events, communities or organisations is purely coincidental.

The author asserts the moral right to be identified as the author of this work.

All rights reserved. No part of this publication may be reproduced, stored in a retrieval system, or transmitted, in any form or by any means, electronic, mechanical, photocopying, recording or otherwise, without the prior written permission of the Publishers.

Dedicated to
All the true lovers in the world.

Acknowledgements

This is my seventh book. I would like to take a moment to thank all the people who became a reason behind this novel and to those who continue to play an important role in my life.

I extend my heartfelt thanks to:

My parents - Sri Suresh Fakkad and Smt Kanti Singh.

My in-laws - Sri Amarnath Singh and Smt Prema Singh.

My family, in-laws' family, relatives and all my friends for being there to support me through thick and thin.

All my readers, fans, well-wishers and critics.

All my gurus.

My editor, Stuti. The kind of work you have done to make this novel better is commendable. I thank you from the bottom of my heart.

The entire team at Srishti Publishers, for bringing the book out.

My wife and best friend, Sunita Singh. Life is simply beautiful with you.

[1]

Our mathematics teacher Manohar Tripathi sir was taking a class. He had announced a surprise test which created panic among the students. Nobody was in a mood for a test; the least of all, me. But what could poor students like us do other than curse Tripathi sir in our heads? We were given forty minutes to complete it. I remembered a dialogue from Shah Rukh Khan's movie *Chak De.*

'Sattar minute, sattar minute hain tumhare paas... tumhari zindagi ke sabse khas sattar minute.'

While Shah Rukh Khan was delivering his power-packed speech in my head, Tripathi sir broke my chain of thoughts, "Your forty minutes start now!"

I was startled out of my reverie. I looked at the whiteboard and quickly scanned all the questions written on it. I was sure I could solve none of them. I had to pass those forty minutes, those accursed forty minutes, though. So with a dispirited mood, I started solving the questions.

"Go back to your seat. Try attempting all the questions. I am not taking any answer sheet until you guys give your best shot."

Tripathi sir's voice caught everyone's attention. I too looked towards the dais. One of the new students in our ninth-class batch, Mohan, was standing there, holding out his copy to Tripathi sir.

"Sir, I am done with all the questions," replied Mohan.

I looked at my watch. Ten minutes were still remaining out of the forty. Mohan seemed to be sprinkling salt on everyone's wounds. Here, I wasn't able to solve even one question, and there was this boy called Mohan submitting his copy ten minutes before time, and also claiming that he had attempted all the questions.

Where the hell has he come from? I wondered.

Tripathi sir stared at Mohan from head to toe. He then took his copy and turned its pages over to check if he had actually solved all the questions. Seconds later, he nodded and signalled to Mohan to go back to his seat. I shook my head in disgust at Mohan and concentrated on my copy as I tried to solve a polynomial equation.

Why the hell did man invent maths at all? I murmured to myself.

"Time is up!" Tripathi sir's hoarse voice caused my ears to itch. I let out a sigh of relief. I desperately wanted the time to be over. He asked the class monitor to collect all the copies and give them to him. After the class was over, the students kicked up a noise-storm, gossiping about Tripathi sir being reprimanded by his wife at home. Meanwhile, Mohan became popular for being the first student to submit his copy. He made many new friends that day. I, however, was jealous of him.

[2]

The next day, the results of the test were announced. Mohan had scored twenty out of twenty marks, while I had scored a big zero. In fact, not only me, but half of the class was awarded with a zero. After Mohan came our previous class topper, Mahendra. He had scored sixteen. Mohan became not only Tripathi sir's favourite, but also of the entire class for his sharp mind. I felt more insulted. Had he been not there, it would have been a usual thing for me. But a new student scoring twenty on twenty against your zero was bound to hurt anyone's ego. I didn't speak to anyone the whole day, which was quite contrary to my nature, the chatterbox that I was.

My best friend Reena asked me during lunch time, "What happened to you? Are you alright?"

"Yeah. I am okay," I replied.

"You don't seem so, but anyway..."

During the day, I stole many glances at Mohan. Slightly taller than an average height boy with dark brown eyes and side-parted hair, he didn't appear to be cocky or boastful in nature. I felt like going to him and saying, "I hate maths, and I hate people who are good at maths even more."

Finally, the bad day was over, and I was back home.

In the evening, after I got up from my afternoon nap, I came out into the balcony. It opened towards the huge, open courtyard of our big ancestral house. Birds were chirping from many corners of the house, and one of our helpers was watering the plants. There was a nice aroma of tea arising from the kitchen on the ground floor.

"Get me my tea please, Ranjan bhaiya," I called out from the balcony.

"Ji, didi," acknowledged Ranjan bhaiya from the kitchen. He was one of our trusted helps and was in charge of the evening tea and snacks for all the family members.

I ran my fingers through my silky hair and sat on a swing chair in the balcony. Meanwhile, my grandmother played Lord Krishna's devotional songs in her room on the ground floor.

Govind bolo Hari Gopal bolo,

Radha Raman Hari Gopal bolo...

Soon, Ranjan bhaiya climbed up the stairs to my balcony with a tray of tea and three kinds of biscuits.

"Here is your tea, didi," he said, keeping the tray on the table in front of me.

"How's your daughter's health now, Ranjan bhaiya?" I asked.

"She is much better, now, didi. All because of this family," he said with a smile and folded hands.

"How many times do I need to tell you, Ranjan bhaiya? You don't have to fold your hands in front of me?"

"That's your love for people like us, otherwise who gives a damn to their servants, leave alone their family."

"Okay, okay, you are too much...please go and carry on with your work," I said and picked my cup of tea.

As I was enjoying my tea, I heard an unknown voice in the courtyard. Curiosity made me move towards the edge of the balcony to see who it was. To my utter surprise, it was my classmate, Mohan.

What is he doing here? I wondered. *Has he come to tell my parents that he has scored hundred percent and I have scored zero in the class test?*

My mother came out from her room, hearing his voice. Mohan handed a packet to my mother with a smile on his face. His complexion was dark, but his smile was very innocent and attractive. An additional canine tooth added more charm to his smile.

"What is this, *beta*?" Ma asked.

"Prasad. Ma had organised Satya Narayan katha."

"I see. I haven't seen you before. Where do you live?"

"In the fourth house from yours. In Yadav uncle's house. We have shifted there a month ago as tenants."

"That's nice. What is your name?"

"He is Mohan. He studies in my class," I said from the balcony.

They both looked up at me. Mohan's eyes widened as he saw me, and so did his smile.

"Oh, so you both know each other?" Ma asked.

I nodded.

"Okay. Would you like to have some tea?" she asked Mohan.

"No, aunty. I am fine," Mohan responded politely.

"Come on! Don't be so formal," I interrupted. "Ma, please ask Ranjan bhaiya to send one more cup of tea. Please come upstairs."

I thought it was the best time to interact and know more about him. Mohan pressed his lips against each other and walked towards the stairs to my balcony as Ma went into the kitchen.

Mohan was certainly different from other boys I had met in my life. He was not handsome as per Indian standards. He did not meet the first criteria itself, and that is having a fair complexion. In our country, if you are not fair, you disqualify being called a handsome man or a beautiful woman. Of course, that is a wrong, unfair notion, but that is how it is in our society. But having said that, he was absolutely charming. Right from his big black eyes, to his finely crafted nose, to his smile, he was someone difficult to ignore. I wondered how I hadn't noticed him for the past month in my class.

"Hello," Mohan said and held out his right hand towards me.

"Hi," I shook his hand after thinking for a while. My ego was not allowing me to be friendly with him. How could he score a hundred percent against my zero!

"I didn't know this is your house."

"So, if you knew, would you not have come?" I asked.

Mohan laughed. "Why would you think like that?" he said.

"It was just a thought."

"Don't think too much in life. It takes the fun away. And by the way, a smile will make you look more beautiful."

His remark caught me unawares. I didn't expect him to praise me with such ease. Mohan was so confident. It was almost impossible not to smile at what he had just said.

"See..." Mohan said as I smiled.

I controlled my lips, not letting them display more happiness on my face.

"Have a seat," I pointed at the chair opposite my swinging one.

Ranjan bhaiya came back with another cup of tea and snacks. I thanked him, and he left.

"So, before shifting here, where did you stay?" I asked Mohan.

"We stayed in a nearby village. Papa decided to shift here for our studies."

"What does your father do?"

"He is an LIC agent. He insures lives." He smiled.

"I see. You seem to be very studious. Hey, have your tea, otherwise it will get cold."

He grabbed his cup and spoke, "That's why my family has moved here, leaving behind our village. I don't have any choice other than proving their decision right."

"That's true," I said. "Have some biscuits too."

Mohan looked at me and picked up one.

"You have learnt so many things about me, but you haven't told me anything about yourself," he said.

"Ask me whatever you want to."

"Why do you look so serious all the time?" he asked.

I laughed a fake laugh. "How can you say that? You don't know me even ten percent."

"I am making that statement based on that ten percent."

"You shouldn't judge people so quickly, should you?"

"I am sorry, I am not judging you. And I didn't mean it that way."

I kept quiet. I don't know why, but I liked his company.

"I know, sometimes people happen to say things they do not mean," I said after a while.

Mohan didn't say anything, just smiled. Probably he didn't agree with me.

"Friends? Can we be friends? This way I will be able to know more than ten percent about you."

He extended his hand towards me.

I was in a dilemma whether it would be right or not to accept his friendship so soon. He probably sensed my confusion and withdrew his hand.

"Never mind. You should always follow your intuition. Probably it's too early to initiate this friendship. Okay then, see you." He smiled again.

"Well, can I ask you something?" I asked.

"Yeah, sure."

"Will you help me with mathematics? I am not so good at it, unlike you." I first wanted to fix the mathematics and then think about friendship with him.

"That would be my pleasure," he said with a smile.

"But I want you to come to my house to teach me. Don't worry, I will pay you for that," I said.

"I will come to your house. That's not a problem, but I won't take money for that."

"But why?"

"I am not a professional teacher. If you really want to pay someone, then you should hire a proper tutor." Mohan crossed his arms across his chest.

"Okay, okay, I get that. So, what time suits you in the evening?" I asked him.

"How about six to seven?"

"That time is booked for my music teacher."

"Oh, so, you learn music?"

"Yeah, I love singing."

"Wow! That is great. Why don't you give me a time?" he said.

"Let's do it after seven. Seven to eight."

"That's fine."

"Thanks, Mohan." I smiled, looking at him.

"You're welcome," he said and stood up to leave.

[3]

"Today, we are going to learn how to sing high notes," Gunjan sir said.

Seeing my inclination towards singing, my father had appointed him as my singing teacher. I was very close to my father, and he'd fulfill all my wishes – fair or unfair. In fact, I was the darling of my house. Gunjan sir was in his early fifties. He had dedicated all his life to music.

"Okay, Guru ji," I said.

Gunjan sir started playing the harmonium. He sang the song *'Tu hi re...'* from the movie Bombay to teach me how to modulate voice for high pitch songs.

"Now, you try," he said.

"Tu hi re, tu hi re, tere bina main kaise jiyun

Aajaa re, aajaa re, yun hi tadpa na tu mujhko."

"No, no, no... Meera. You have to stretch a little at *'aaja reee'*. Follow me," he said and sang that line himself.

It took me a few attempts before I got it right.

"Yes... like that. Superb! Now, continue the song," Gunjan sir praised me.

After I finished the song, I drank some water from a glass on the side table. Tea had arrived for Guru ji. He said while taking a sip, "I think now you are ready to participate in competitions like Indian Idol and Sa Re Ga Ma Pa."

"Thank you, Guru ji," I said. "I'd be very excited to be a part of such reality shows."

"I can understand. But keep in mind one thing, Meera. The choice of songs is the key, especially in the audition round."

"You are right, Guru ji. Please help me with the selection of songs. I have come to know from one of my relatives that the audition for a singing show for kids is going to start from next month. And the channel is coming to Gorakhpur as well for an initial screening. This is such a good chance. I don't want to miss it," I said.

"I see. You must try your luck. I will tell my other students to get ready for it as well. We have one month so, don't worry. I will work with you on a few songs. Okay then, that's it for today," Guru ji said and left.

[4]

The next morning, as I entered my classroom, I saw almost all the boys standing on the dais. They were all facing the whiteboard. I kept my bag on my desk and looked questioningly at Reena, my best friend.

"What happened? Why are these monkeys monkeying around?" I asked Reena.

She smiled. "Someone has affixed a poster of Ravana on the board."

"Ravana?" I wondered. "Who is from the Ravana clan here?"

Reena shrugged. I moved forward and said, "Why are you guys making so much noise?"

All the boys turned towards me.

"Rani Laxmibai has come," someone mumbled.

"Who said that?" I questioned, my hands on my waist.

The boys smiled and began stepping down from the dais. I saw Mohan in the crowd as well. He smiled upon seeing me. I felt something as he did so. I replied with a slight smile even though I didn't want to.

I gazed at the board. There was Ravana with his evil laugh on a poster. Someone had drawn the sketch and glued it on the board with the help of transparent tape.

I turned towards the class and narrowed my gaze. "Who is Ravana's fan here?"

"That's the suspense," said Vineet, one of my classmates.

"I can understand, guys. It is not surprising but obvious. Nobody would expect you to draw Rama."

I was lecturing at my classmates when our teacher Kanti ma'am entered the class.

"Good morning, ma'am," the whole class greeted her as I went back to my desk.

"Good morning, students," ma'am acknowledged with a smile. "Are you taking a lecture today, Meera?" she asked me.

"Not really, ma'am. But you certainly have to find who the artist among us is," I said, pointing at the whiteboard.

Kanti ma'am turned to look at the board.

"This is a nice sketch. Who has done this?"

I used to sit in the front row along with my friends Reena and Disha. I looked towards my left and then right to see if someone had raised a hand, but nobody did. I noticed all other students looking towards the last bench of the class. I turned as well.

I couldn't believe Mohan had raised his hand. He was sitting on the last bench with two notorious boys Sanjeev and Ranjeet. He was smiling, and that surprised me.

"Please stand up," ma'am said to him.

Mohan obeyed her.

"So, you sketch?"

"Yes, ma'am," Mohan replied.

"I must say that you are a good artist, but why have you pasted it here?"

"Well, ma'am, sorry about that. But I didn't find a better way to showcase my talent to the entire class," Mohan replied.

"I see. But this is indiscipline, Mohan. Since you are new in the school, I am letting it go this time, but please make sure that you don't repeat this in future. And why Ravana? Do you like him?"

"Yes, ma'am. I like him."

The entire class booed as he said that. *Has he gone mad?* I wondered.

Ma'am shushed the students and crossed her hands across her chest.

"For the first time someone says that he likes Ravana," ma'am said.

"Ma'am, I like him because if he was not there, who would Lord Rama kill? I like him because I like adharma being defeated," Mohan said.

Now, that answer surprised me. This boy was certainly different. He was not only charming by his looks, but his words were also something to ponder about.

"That's interesting. But unfortunately, it is not a philosophy period, but English. So, can you please remove this so that I can start my lecture?" ma'am said.

"It's really difficult for me to tear it off since it is my own creation. Could you ask somebody else to remove this, ma'am? I am s... sorry," Mohan said.

The entire classroom filled with laughter. Mohan seemed to have offended Kanti ma'am. I don't know why, but I wanted to be on his side. So, before ma'am could take any possible action against him, I said, "Let me do it."

I climbed up the dais and reached out to the poster. I carefully took it off the board. And as I did so, I found another poster underneath it. And this was another surprise. A beautiful sketch of Lord Rama was pasted there. I turned towards the class with the poster of Ravana in my hand.

"*Wow!*" The entire classroom exclaimed in unison. The next moment some of the boys chanted 'Jai Shree Ram!' and rest of the class followed.

I looked at Mohan. He was flashing his extra canine teeth. I must admit his smile made me feel attracted towards him.

"Okay, so here is the suspense," Kanti ma'am said.

"Yes, ma'am. In order to see Lord Rama, you have to kill Ravana," Mohan said. "Please take that poster off too, Meera, so that ma'am can start," he said to me.

"Yeah, sure." I removed Lord Rama's poster with extreme care.

"Let's have a round of applause for Mohan. But please, Mohan, don't do it again. We are aware of your talent now," Kanti ma'am said.

I could not focus on what ma'am taught us that day. I kept thinking about Mohan. I wondered what kind of guy he was! For the first time in my life, I was curious about someone.

[5]

The next day, as the lunch break bell rang, Sanjeev sir stopped his lecture and the boys started moving out of the classroom. We too went to washroom and came back after washing our hands. I sat on my seat and moved my hand inside my bag to take my lunchbox out.

Where is it? I wondered, my eyes on my bag. It was not there. I checked all the other sections of my bag, but didn't find it anywhere.

What the hell! Where is my lunchbox? Did Ma forget to keep it in my bag? But if she did, why would she say that she had given me my favourite noodles.

"What happened, Meera?" Disha asked me.

I looked at her with a sad face. "My tiffin is not here."

"Who has taken it? I am sure it is the job of these mischievous guys," she said.

I darted my glance around the classroom. Most of the students were eating their food. I then rivetted my gaze towards the last bench where Mohan sat.

What the hell! Mohan was eating noodles along with Sanjeev and Ranjeet. My rage knew no bounds. I went straight up to him.

He looked up at me, with the strands of noodles hanging out from his mouth. He grinned sheepishly and sucked them in. He then picked up my tiffin box and held it out towards me.

"It's delicious. Who made it?" he asked.

"How dare you steal my lunchbox?" I asked in anger, my hands on my hips.

"Actually, I was very hungry. I checked out a few other lunch boxes, but there was nothing different. Then I came across yours and found these noodles. I am sorry, but noodles are my favourite. I couldn't help myself," Mohan replied sheepishly.

"If you are hungry, why aren't you eating your own lunch?"

"Well, I haven't brought my lunch today."

"So, am I responsible for that?"

"No. Absolutely not."

"Then why am I being punished?" I hissed.

"I am sorry... I just wanted to taste a little, but inadvertently I seem to have eaten quite a bit." He glanced at the tiffin box.

"This is not done, Mohan. Now what will I eat?" I asked.

"Some of it is still there."

"I don't eat leftover food. And I hate you, Mohan." I turned and came back to my desk in a huff.

Disha and Reena offered their lunches to me, but my mood was off. I refused. I heard the sound of noodles being slurped and that only made me angrier.

This guy has no manners. How could he steal my lunch?

I stood up and walked out of the classroom. I went to the central garden of our school and sat on the grounds. Disha and Reena came after me.

"I told you, no? I don't feel like eating now. You please have your lunch," I said as they came and sat beside me.

"Let's first eat and then decide how to teach this insolent guy a lesson," said Disha as she opened her tiffin box.

I nodded. I couldn't pretend that I wasn't hungry any longer seeing the parathas, and we shared them between us.

Before the lunch break was over, we came back to our classroom. We had our history class next, right after recess. I quickly glanced at Mohan's desk. He was not there.

Soon, our history teacher Vinod Rai entered the classroom and started taking attendance. Mohan had not come yet. Vinod sir called his name.

Where has he gone? I thought. *Always creating some or the other problem. First, he ate my noodles, and now only god knows where he has gone.*

I was unable to focus on the lecture.

Ten minutes before the lecture was about to end, my eyes fell upon Mohan. He stood outside the class.

"May I come in, sir?" he asked Vinod sir.

Much to my surprise, my tiffin box was in his hands. *What the hell has he been doing with my tiffin box*?

Vinod sir looked at him and then at his wrist watch. "Where are you coming from, Mister?"

"Sorry, sir. I had some personal work."

"Personal work?" Vinod sir asked, surprised.

"Yes, sir."

"May I know what personal work did you have?"

"It wouldn't remain personal if I tell you about it, sir" Mohan said.

The whole class laughed. Vinod sir was offended.

"My class is not a garden that you can walk in any time you feel like," he said. "Come to the principal's room after the class is over."

"Okay, sir." Mohan smiled.

Vinod sir taught for five more minutes and left.

"Meet me in the principal's room," he said to Mohan before leaving.

He nodded and immediately came to my desk. He kept my tiffin box on the desk and smiled, looking into my eyes.

"Sorry," he said. "I realised I should have taken your permission before eating your noodles."

"That's okay," I said. Somehow my anger melted away.

He opened the lid of my tiffin box. It was filled with Maggi. I couldn't believe it.

"What is this?" I exclaimed.

"Maggi."

"That I can see. I mean where did you get it from?"

"I will tell you everything. But first, you have to accept it," said Mohan.

I felt embarrassed. I had scolded him for eating my noodles, and this guy had got Maggi for me.

I laughed. "I am sorry. I shouldn't have reacted that way."

"That was totally natural," Mohan said. "Hey, I will be back. Vinod sir will be waiting for me."

"Oh, why did you go to get Maggi in the middle of the lecture?" I asked.

"I will be back," he said with a hint of smile on his lips, and left.

I looked at my friends and asked them to share my Maggi. They didn't refuse the special treat.

[6]

I was walking towards our red Mercedes parked just outside our school. My father had bought this car for me and it was at my disposal. My father Ratan Singh Rajpoot was probably the best lawyer in Gorakhpur. And being the best lawyer obviously meant great wealth. You can say I was born with a golden spoon, and thus I never cared about money.

I bade goodbye to my friends Disha and Reena. Just then my eyes fell upon Mohan who was cackling with his friends on his way out of school.

I called out to him, "Mohan!"

He glanced around to see who had called him. As he looked at me, he waggled his eyebrows. I gestured at him to come over.

"Yes, Meera. What happened?" he asked. He always seemed to be happy.

"You didn't tell me where you got the Maggi from?" I asked.

"Well, I went to our peon Chhangu's quarter and requested him to allow me to use his kitchen. He is a nice man. I also borrowed money from him for a packet of Maggi. He lent me that as well. That's the story."

"Are you nuts? What was the need for all this?"

"Arrey, I had finished your noodles so it was my responsibility to arrange food for you."

"You're crazy, Mohan. What else can I say?" I smiled. I was

impressed by what he did for me. “Anyway, when are you planning to start my maths tuitions?”

“Today I have to go to Nusrat’s birthday party. So, from tomorrow?”

“Nusrat who? Our classmate?” I quizzed, my brows coming closer.

“Yes, it’s her birthday today,” Mohan said.

“I know. She distributed cake in the class. But why has she invited you to her house?” I felt a pang of jealousy.

“That’s difficult for me to answer,” Mohan flashed his canines.

“Are you going?”

“Of course. If I don’t go, wouldn’t it look rude?”

“Why rude? It’s your choice whether you want to go or not,” I suggested. I didn’t want Mohan to go to Nusrat’s birthday party.

“Well, I want to go. I love birthday feasts and she is my friend.”

“And who am I?”

“You are also a friend. So, if you invite me to your birthday party, then I would come as well,” he said.

“Didn’t she invite you?” he asked me.

“No. And even if she did, I wouldn’t go.”

“Why?”

I moved my eyes away from him. “Because she is not my friend.”

He shrugged. “Okay then, see you,” he said.

“See you,” I said angrily and headed towards my car.

[7]

Mohan was extremely popular and was always surrounded by boys and girls. The next day when I entered my classroom, I saw many students surrounding him while he was holding a girl's hand.

What is he up to now? I wondered, keeping my bag onto my desk. I asked Reena, "What is this?"

She replied, "He is predicting the future."

"What nonsense! How can one predict somebody's future?" I babbled and walked up to his desk.

"Why are you making a fool of these guys?" I said.

Mohan looked up at me with his signature smile. "Some people don't believe in it, but palmistry is backed by science."

"Bullshit!" I exclaimed.

"You want to try it out?"

"I can't say about others, but Mohan knows it well for sure. A lot of things he said about me are hundred percent true," said Nusrat.

I glared at her. "Huh!" I said and came back to my seat.

Ravi, one of my classmates, drew my attention. "He is not a good guy."

I turned back to look at him. "Why?"

"He is only pretending that he knows palmistry so that he gets a chance to hold girls' hands."

"Really?" I quizzed.

"Yes. That's why when a boy shows him his hand, he sees it only for a minute or two. But when a girl does so, he doesn't let go for five minutes," Ravi said.

I stole a quick glance at Mohan. He was still holding the same girl's hand. I didn't like this.

Why are all the students of the class so fond of him? I thought. *You are also fond of him. Aren't you?* A voice arose in me.

No, I am not fond of him. Another voice within me denied the allegation.

"Good morning, students," Kanti ma'am greeted the students as she entered the classroom.

Everyone went back to their desks.

*

"You really know palmistry?" I asked Mohan.

He had come home to teach me mathematics as promised. We were sitting around my study table in my room.

He beamed at me. "Give me your hand," he asked.

I shook my head. "I don't believe in it."

"But you want to believe, don't you?"

I don't know what happened, but my heart began beating faster. I felt nervous.

> *Yes, Meera Singh Rajpoot was nervous. The one who never became nervous in front of anyone in her life. Not even then when a group of boys had stopped her one afternoon on an empty road while she was going to the Krishna temple in the outskirts of the city. She had slapped their leader. A few passersby had also gathered there, forcing the boys to run away.*
>
> *But today when a dark-complexioned boy was asking for her hand, a boy who was her classmate, she was nervous. How could he be so authoritative?*

"Our classmates say that you do this so that you can hold girls' hands," I said.

Mohan laughed. "Okay, let us focus on mathematics then. Palmistry is not in our course."

What does this guy think of himself? Why does he act so pricey? I said inside my head. *Is he not interested in holding my hand?*

"No, first you have to see my hand and tell me about my future," I said. "How can you say 'no' to me?"

"I didn't say 'no' to you."

"Then tell me what is there in my future?" I extended my hand towards him.

Mohan didn't hold my hand, but started looking at my palm.

"You can hold my hand," I said.

He looked up at me and smiled. "No, that's okay. I can see the lines very clearly."

This guy never leaves a chance to annoy, I mumbled.

"If you want to do it, do it properly, otherwise just let it be," I said and withdrew my hand.

Just then he caught my hand and opened my palm with the other hand of his. I felt the warmth of his hand and my heart skipped a beat.

He read my hand and I read his face. His curly hair would be quite long if made straight. A mole on his left cheek only added to his charm.

"So, what do you see?" I asked.

"I am no expert, but I can say you're special."

My lips widened into a smile as he said that.

"As in?"

"First of all, you have an artist hidden in you. Is that right?" he asked.

"Yes, I am a singer."

"One day you will be famous all over the world."

"Really?"

"Yes."

"Is that written on my hand?" I asked.

"That is what lines on your hand suggest."

"How long am I going to live?"

"Very long. Probably forever."

"*Dhat!* How can anyone live forever?"

"Through one's deeds. You will be alive even after you leave this body," Mohan said.

"You say such profound things," I said.

"That's all I have to say."

"Wait! What about my love-life?" I asked.

"Very adventurous."

"Meaning?"

"Meaning there'll be lots of ups and downs."

"That is fine. In fact, that's what life is."

"Absolutely right."

"What else do you see?" I was more curious.

"You have a big heart. People around you will always be happy," he added.

"Thank you. What else?"

"A lot of challenges will come your way, but you are a fighter. You'll be able to tackle them."

"I see. What else?"

"What else do you want to hear?" Mohan said with a smile.

"You tell me."

"Life is a mystery. You should live it," he said. "Now, let's talk about maths."

"Yep," I said and opened my book.

"So, where do we start?" he asked.

"I find it difficult to calculate volumes of cubes and cuboids."

"Okay, let me help you with it," he said and opened the page that talked about cubes.

[8]

Two Years Later

Our twelfth board exams were scheduled a month later. Mohan still frequented my house for tuitions. My friendship with him had come a long way and we were best friends now. To be honest, I had started liking him as well. If someone else had been in his place, he would have certainly tried to take advantage of the situation. But Mohan was different. He never let me know what was there in his heart for me. Probably, the right time had not yet come.

I had been asking him to come with me for an outing for a long time. But he always put it off. I knew the reason for his refusal. An outing with me meant a lot of expenditure. That's why he used to make up some or the other excuse every time. But this time, I had forced him emotionally, making him swear upon me. Finally, he had agreed.

We had come to Kushmi forest. It is the biggest green area covered with trees in Gorakhpur. I had worn a pista-coloured top along with neon blue denim pants. Mohan was clad in a crisp white shirt with a pair of blue denim pants. He was carrying his guitar as well which I had gifted him on his last birthday. He didn't have any formal training, but he was really good at it. Whatever he knew, he had learnt from YouTube videos. I had heard him first in our school when he had played one of our classmate's guitar.

There were not many people in Kushumi forest. This was the first time when just two of us had come alone somewhere. The fear of being seen by some of my father's acquaintances pestered me. But then I thought if I kept fearing like that, I would not be able to enjoy my outing with Mohan.

A few times, our eyes met, and we exchanged smiles. It was a completely different feeling. We were talking less, but still enjoyed each other's company. We were walking on a road in the forest. A few couples were walking ahead of us, oblivious to the world around them. The long trees on both sides of the road had covered most of it. Sunlight filtered through the gap between the dense leaves of the trees as the cool breeze of February caressed our faces. I felt something and couldn't stop myself from asking Mohan.

"Can I hold your hand?"

Mohan looked at me with a smile mixed with surprise. "Yes, you can."

I blushed and entwined my fingers between his. The feeling of his warm hand made my heart flutter. A ripple of joy ran through my body.

We are no longer just friends. Let's admit that. I wanted to tell Mohan, but did not. After all, it was his job to do so.

We kept walking hand in hand and went further into the forest. We came across a big rock on the right side of the road.

"Let's rest. I am tired," I said.

Mohan nodded. We sat on that rock.

I opened the cap of the water bottle I was carrying and drank some water from it. I asked Mohan if he was thirsty too. He nodded and took the bottle from me.

"It's so pleasant here. Isn't it?" I asked him.

"Absolutely. You don't breathe such fresh air in town and hear the songs of the birds," he said after taking a swig of the water.

I smiled, gazing at him.

"So, when is your singing audition?" he asked.

"A week after our last exam, on Sunday," I said. "Last time I missed it because I had dengue. Do you know how many days I mourned over it?"

Mohan bobbed his head. "Ten days, continuously. You have told me many times."

"I can't miss it this time, come what may."

"You won't miss it," he said.

"How come?"

"I know."

"Okay. You have to come with me to the audition," I said.

"Are you sure? Would your family like it?"

"Umm... you are right. Ma will be there with me for sure. So what? You can still come to support me, can't you?"

Mohan looked at me and smiled.

"Okay, what do you think? Will I win the competition?" I asked.

"Why not? You have not let anyone win a single singing competition held in Gorakhpur in the past three years. I don't have a bit of doubt."

"Thanks, Mohan. You have shot my confidence to the sky. I wonder if I'll be able to perform and win the competition."

"Don't worry about the results. You only focus on giving your hundred percent," he said.

"Sometimes, you talk like Lord Krishna," I said.

"That's who I am. Mohan!" He flashed his extra tooth once again.

By that logic, I am your lover. Meera! I thought and smiled. I smiled because I felt I was really in love with Mohan.

Mohan laughed and took the guitar out of the bag. He held it, keeping it on his right thigh, and strummed it a few times. He then shifted a little to turn towards me, as I kept my chin on my palm, with my elbow on my right thigh. His lips curved into a charming smile as he started singing.

Ho..
Ye raaten ab nahi dhadaktin
Din bhi saans nahi lete
Ab to aa jao mere soneya
Baaten rah gayin adhoori
Mere labon pe zaroori
Aake sun jao mere soneya
Tere bin… nahi laage jiyaa
Tere bin… ab to aa ja piyaa
Tere bin… nahi laage jiyaa …aa

"You sing so well. Why don't you participate with me in the competitions?" I asked as Mohan finished the song.

"Hah! Sometimes, you do exaggerate, Meera. I sing well only in front of you, but my voice is not that good," Mohan said.

"And sometimes, you underplay your talent, Mohan. Your voice is not that bad," I said.

"I don't want to be your competition." Mohan laughed.

"I would love to have tough competition."

"Just let it be, Meera. Tell me, how's your sister?" Mohan changed the topic.

"Archana is fine and enjoying college life," I said.

"Jungle me oye oye!"

An unknown voice startled me. I looked in the direction from where the voice had come. Three boys dressed up like loafers appeared from behind a huge peepal tree.

I looked at Mohan, who smiled and asked me to keep calm as the boys approached us. One of them said, "What the hell are you guys doing here?"

"Don't you know what this is?" Mohan said, keeping the guitar in the bag.

"Guitar," one of them replied.

"So?" The first boy asked again, keeping his hands on his hips.

"What does one do with a guitar?" Mohan asked, zipping up the bag.

"Play songs," the other boy said.

"Shut up!" the first boy scolded his friend. "Are you playing KBC with him that you're answering all his questions?"

And then he turned to us. "I am talking about you two. People like you are spoiling the name of Gorakhpur."

"How come, brother? Would you please explain?" Mohan kept the bag aside and asked.

"You guys come into the jungle to romance each other and make it filthy," the boy said.

"So, according to you, romance is filthy?" Mohan asked.

"Yes," the boy gave a stern reply.

"If that is so, you are filth yourself. Because you are the product of the romance between your parents," Mohan said.

"Bastard!" The boy lunged at Mohan and caught his collar.

Mohan shoved his hand away and said, "Listen, I am calling you brother. And you are holding my collar. You think that is the right behaviour?"

"How dare you abuse my parents?" The boy's eyes turned red.

"Looks like you are dumb. You have difficulty understanding simple things," Mohan said. I laughed at his remark.

"He speaks too much. Let's teach the bastard a lesson." The third boy who was standing near me caught my hand.

I screamed.

Mohan looked at him. "Leave her hand."

"What will you do if I don't," he replied.

"I request you," Mohan said.

"I decline your request."

"See, I don't like violence. But I don't hesitate doing it if there is no option left," Mohan said.

The boy smiled and kept his other hand on my waist. I felt like slapping him hard, but restrained from doing so. I wanted to see what Mohan would do.

Mohan came closer to us and slapped the boy. The resounding sound was testimony to how hard it was. He immediately released me and charged at Mohan. But Mohan was ready for the counter attack. He swiftly moved to his right and evaded that boy's punch. Mohan then caught his collar and gave him a few slaps. Just then, another boy struck Mohan on his back with his fist. The struggle between Mohan and the three boys began. I had never seen Mohan fighting. But he was quite fierce and quick, taking on all of them on his own.

I could not be a spectator, and therefore, I looked around for something that could be my weapon. I found one wooden stick. I picked it and hit one of the guys with it. He turned to look back at me while the other two continued fighting with Mohan. I hit him a few more times, but the stick wasn't thick enough to cause any harm. He pounced at me. Mohan was watching his actions. Before that boy could touch me, Mohan kicked him really hard and he fell face down. Mohan turned to the other boys and slapped them alternately.

I had never imagined Mohan could be this strong. Although he himself had been at the receiving end of quite a few kicks and punches, he didn't allow those scoundrels to take any advantage. Eventually, when they realised they couldn't defeat Mohan, they started abusing us vocally.

"We will be watching you," their leader said.

"Get lost!" Mohan said, smoothening the wrinkles on his shirt with his hand.

One of them took his mobile out and clicked a picture of us.

"What the hell!" I exclaimed worriedly.

Mohan sprinted towards them, but they ran away like a group of deer running for their lives.

"Why did they take our picture?" I asked, concerned, as Mohan came back.

"Out of frustration. What else?"

"I am sorry, Mohan. I shouldn't have forced you to come here," I said.

"Hey, why sorry? You didn't invite them, right?"

"I know, but..."

Mohan patted me on the back. "Don't worry. Let's complain to the security here."

I nodded.

Will they use this picture against us? I thought. *How can they? There is nothing in that. Can they show this picture to my family? If yes, what will I tell them?*

All these thoughts were troubling me when Mohan complained to the security at the main entrance of the park. My first outing with Mohan had been completely spoiled. There was no point in staying there. Mohan accompanied me home, but didn't get out of the cab. I had tears in my eyes when he departed. All I wanted was a good time with him, but it had ended up otherwise.

[9]

"I can understand you went to enjoy your Sunday. But why didn't you tell anyone in the family?" my father said.

I stood in my father's meeting room at our house at 8 p.m. where I had been summoned.

How the hell did Papa came to know about it? I wondered. *Did those guys send him the picture they had taken? But how did they know who my father is?*

"He is my friend, Papa. Can't I go out with him?" I asked.

"Of course, you can. But when the family doesn't know about such outings and comes to know about it from people outside, it's not right. I hope you understand, Meera."

"I do, Papa. Who told you, by the way?" I asked.

"Doesn't matter. What really matters is that you tell me about it."

I looked up at my father. He was an elegant man with clean-shaven look, well combed salt-and-pepper hair, and deep eyes. I felt really bad that I had caused him unnecessary trouble. But he should have also understood that not everything can be shared with one's parents.

"I am sorry, Papa," I said after a while.

"I am sure you won't repeat such things," he said in response to my apology.

I will make sure you never get to know such things, I said in my head and nodded.

"And what does this guy's family do?" Papa asked, taking his spectacles off.

"Well, his father works for an insurance company," I said.

"Insurance agent?" Papa quizzed.

I nodded.

He kept his glasses on a side table.

"Let me hire a professional tutor for you," he said.

"No, Papa. He is really good at maths. And he has been teaching me for the past two years," I said quickly.

Papa looked at me for a while and said, "Okay, if you say so."

"Thank you, Papa," I said.

Papa smiled. I smiled in response, though I didn't know if something was hidden behind Papa's smile.

"Mohan bhaiya, sir is calling you," Ranjan bhaiya called out from the door of my room.

Mohan and I, both looked up at him from my Calculus book. Mohan turned his gaze at me and raised his eyebrows.

"I told you, that he has come to know about our outing to Kushmi forest," I said.

"I see," Mohan said.

"Okay, I am coming," he said to Ranjan bhaiya.

I caught Mohan's hand as he stood up to leave. He narrowed his gaze at me, a smile on his lips.

"Promise, you will tell me everything he says to you in detail," I said.

"Why are you worried?"

"I don't know."

"Relax, Meera."

"I will, after you make the promise."

"Okay, I promise," he said. "Now, solve question number nine."

I nodded and gave him directions to the meeting room on the ground floor.

Half an hour later, Mohan came back. I heaved a sigh of relief. I wanted to know if he was upset, but I must say Mohan is a very composed man. His expressions didn't reveal much about what had happened in my father's room.

"What happened, Mohan?" I couldn't hold my horses.

"Nothing much. Your father is a very nice man," Mohan said, sitting in his chair.

Is it a sarcastic remark or a true observation? I wondered.

"What did he tell you?" I asked, curious.

"He asked me what happened in Kushmi forest?"

"So, what did you say?"

"I told him everything that had happened."

"And what did he say?" I asked.

"He said the obvious. We should have told our families about this trip. We are not yet adults. Just seventeen."

"Hmm... what else?"

"He said he will make sure the culprits are punished."

"Did he scold you as well?" I expressed my biggest concern.

Mohan shook his head, though unconvincingly.

"Look at me, Mohan," I said to him as he dug into the Calculus book.

I closed the book. He looked at me, serious expressions on his face.

"What happened, Mohan? Did Papa say something to you?" I asked.

"You're unnecessarily worried. We did nothing wrong for which he would reprimand me."

"I know. I am just asking."

"No, he just asked me to behave in a more mature way," he said.

"What does 'more-mature-way' mean?"

"Come on, Meera! Don't talk like a kid," he said.

For the first time, I sensed tension in Mohan's voice.

"Did you solve question number nine?" he asked to avert the topic.

I shook my head in denial.

"Why?"

"I am doing it now," I replied like an obedient student.

"Give me the book."

He took the book from me and marked a few more questions.

"Do these integration problems as well. That's your homework for today." And he stood up to leave.

"What happened?" I looked up at him, puzzled.

"I have to go. It's already a quarter past eight," he said.

Something had definitely happened. He was not in the right mood to discuss anything. There was no point. I decided to let go for the moment. However, I wasn't happy with my father. If visiting Kushmi forest was wrong, then the fault was mine, and there was no need to hold Mohan responsible.

[10]

One Month Later

Our twelfth board exams were over in the month of April. The last paper was on a Friday. The following Sunday, the audition for the singing competition was being held. Mohan's birthday was also around the corner.

Our entire class decided to go on a picnic the day after our last exam. After brainstorming for about half of a day on our WhatsApp group, we finalised Neer Nikunj water park as the destination. The weather had also become warmer since last month, and thus everybody voted for it.

I was very excited on Saturday morning. I had never been to a water park with my friends before. I packed my swim suit and two pairs of underclothes for the water park. I put in a sunscreen lotion along with the other items of my make up including my favourite perfume from Gucci. I was choosing from pairs of jeans and t-shirts to change later when my sister, Archana entered my room.

"Where are you going, di?" she asked.

I glanced at her and smiled. "Water park."

"Really! That's amazing."

"Yeah," I said. "You tell me."

"Well, can Mohan teach me mathematics?" she asked.

I stopped midway folding my clothes and looked at her. "Why? You're already taking turions from Akhilendra sir, right?"

"Yeah, but he is only good till tenth standard. Although, he teaches eleventh and twelfth standard students, he is not good enough."

"I see." I thought for a while.

My twelfth is over. And I have no interest studying maths for my graduation. In fact, I would have left it just after my tenth if Mohan was not there. I'll pass in maths only because of him. Now, there would be no reason for Mohan to come to my house every day. I was already sad because of this fact. Archana wants to learn from him and that is like a boon in disguise. Mohan would be coming home for the next two years. What else could I ask for?

"What happened, di? Is there a problem?" Archana interrupted my thoughts.

"Absolutely not!" I said, startled. "But I need to ask Mohan about it."

"Sure. Let me know," Archana said, passing me the stack of clothes that I had already folded.

I nodded with a smile. "Thanks."

"Enjoy your day," she said and left my room.

"I can't do anymore," I said, sitting on the poolside platform, after doing four slides consecutively. Water was streaming down my hair.

"Come on, Meera! How can you get tired so soon?" Mohan caught my hand and pulled me up.

"I am seriously tired, Mohan," I looked at his bare abdomen. He had prominent six pack abs. I had to admit I felt attracted.

"You don't come to a water park to get tired." He took me to another spiral slide.

Chhapak!

We fell into a five feet deep water pool where the slide ended. The water level touched my chin. I tilted my head up and asked for Mohan's hand. He gave me his right hand. As I came closer to him, he kept his left hand on my waist and walked me towards the edge of the pool. Ripples of joy went through my whole body.

Mohan rested against the wall of the pool, keeping his arms onto the upper surface that met the floor, his face up at a thirty-degree angle. I too stood beside him. The water park was flooded with people since it was Saturday. There was a queue of five to six people in front of every slide. Most of the students had divided themselves into groups.

"Spare some time with us also, Mohan," Nusrat said as she passed by us with her friends.

Her friends giggled.

Mohan smiled. "Of course, why don't you join us?"

"Why don't you join us," Nusrat said. "We are going to the Lazy Pool."

Mohan looked at me. "Not bad. Let's join them."

I pulled Mohan's hand under water. "Let them go. We shall join them later."

"Okay," Mohan said.

"You girls proceed, we shall join you in some time," I said to Nusrat and her friends.

They didn't say anything in response, just giggled.

Let me confess. By then, my classmates had started speculating that there was something brewing between Mohan and me, although there was no confession from us.

"My sister Archana wants you to teach her maths," I said as we relaxed. I had put on my sunglasses.

"What?" exclaimed Mohan, giving me a glance sideways.

"Yes. She asked me today morning."

"You know I am not a professional tutor. I taught you only because..." He stopped mid-sentence.

"Because?" My gaze narrowed at him.

Droplets of perspiration on his face shone in the sunlight.

"Because you are my friend," he added.

"And she is your friend's sister." I beamed.

I wish I could tell him that it was me who wanted him to teach my sister more than my sister herself, because that way I could see him every day at home for two more years.

"Okay." Mohan agreed.

Just then, a whistle was blown. It meant time for the wavy pool, a pool where they create waves like those of the sea.

"Time for wavy pool. Let's go, Meera," Mohan climbed up the floor and extended his hand towards me.

I smiled and held it as I came out of the pool.

They played latest Bollywood dance songs by the pool side. I noticed many couples in the wavy pool with their arms around each other. I too wanted the same intimacy with Mohan, but it was not possible. We were not a couple yet. We joined our classmates and enjoyed the waves. Mohan took me deeper in the pool and instructed me to jump with him as the huge waves neared us.

We headed to the rain dance floor next where we danced for quite some time. The outing was real fun and a much-needed break after our exams.

[11]

I had already decided what I wanted to gift Mohan for his birthday. An iPhone. I went and bought it from an authorised Apple store near my house and got it prettily packed with red gift-wrapping paper. When you are in love, red automatically becomes your favourite colour.

Finally, the day had come. The party was at seven p.m. on the terrace of Mohan's house. I choose a fuchsia coloured lehenga for the occasion.

"How do I look?" I asked Archana, gazing at myself in the dressing mirror. She had just come into my room wearing a light green Anarkali suit. Mohan had invited her as well.

She made an expression that had a question mark along with a sly smile?

Does she also doubt me? I thought to myself.

She made an 'O' with her thumb and index finger. "Beautiful, my lovely sister," she said.

"Thank you, my little sister. I love you," I blushed at her compliment.

"So, you ready?" she asked me.

"Yeah, just ten more minutes," I said, looking for my mascara.

"Okay. Call me when you are ready to leave," she said and left.

Finally, I applied my light pink lip gloss and smiled at myself. My hair stylist had already given me a wavy hairstyle.

I stood up from my dressing stool and applied some perfume on my neck and pulse points. And there I was, ready for the party. The birthday party of the boy I loved.

Around twenty people sang together as Mohan cut the cake.

Happy birthday to you,
Happy birthday to you,
Happy birthday, dear Mohan,
Happy birthday to you.

The ambience was fantastic on his terrace. Along the parapet, they had fixed low wattage warm light bulbs that produced a lovely golden light. The terrace was lined with plants in lovely earthen planters. I stood with my sister, clapping for Mohan. He first fed the cake to his parents and then looked at me. He gestured to me to come to him. I hesitated a little, wondering what people would think about me.

Am I the most important person in Mohan's life after his parents? He wants to feed me cake? What would my own sister think? People anyway suspect we are together, despite the fact that we are still just friends. Like best friends.

"Meera."

Mohan's voice caught my attention. I came out of my thoughts and went to him.

"I should feed you. It's your birthday, Mohan," I said.

"Later. First, open your mouth," he said excitedly, bringing the cake to my mouth.

I had no choice, but to open my mouth to let the cake in, which was already touching my lips. I took a slice myself and fed Mohan back.

"Happy birthday," I whispered to him, gazing into his black eyes.

"Thanks, dear Meera," he replied, eating the cake. He was dressed up in a yellow Indo-western kurta and a loose pyjama. His curly hair shone in that soft light while the soft hair had become prominent on his moustache line. His mother had applied a *teeka* on his forehead.

"This is for you," I held out my gift to him.

"What's that?"

"Your birthday gift."

"What is the need of this formality?"

"For me, it's a way of expressing my emotions, not a formality," I said.

Mohan flashed his charismatic smile which made my heart skip a beat.

"Let me also feed you," one of Mohan's neighbours interjected our conversation.

"Of course," I said and stepped back.

Mohan was surrounded by many of his friends who proceeded to smear his face with icing.

I had developed feelings for Mohan. For me, it was not merely friendship between us. It was more. But I didn't know what Mohan thought about us.

Was he also in love with me? Sometimes, it seemed so. Sometimes, it didn't. When will he propose his love to me? Will he ever? What is he afraid of? Is it the difference in the status of our families? I was talking to myself when Mohan announced.

"Let me introduce my best friend to you all. She is Meera – the best singer in Gorakhpur."

People clapped, but I felt awkward. Why did Mohan have to introduce me like that? His next statement answered my question.

"I would like to request her to sing a song for us."

I was startled by the announcement.

"What is this, Mohan?" I said.

"Come on, Meera!"

I couldn't refuse those pleading eyes.

"Okay," I said.

"Get a chair for her," Mohan asked one of his cousins.

"Don't worry, I will play the guitar for you," Mohan said to me and went to get his guitar.

Meanwhile, the people gathered around me. Some of them stood leaning against the parapet, while others sat on chairs. Another chair was placed beside mine for Mohan. My sister Archana gave me a thumbs up and I smiled softly.

"So, which song?" Mohan looked at me, while strumming the guitar chords.

"You suggest one," I said as a refreshing breeze brought some respite on the hot evening.

Mohan shook his head. "I want you to choose."

"Okay, let me think." I thought of a song which would express my feelings for Mohan as well. Probably, then he would understand me. Our eyes met few times, and we smiled.

"Okay, you have heard the song – *Mainu ishq tera le dooba*, right?" I asked Mohan.

"The one featuring Siddarth Malhotra and Rakul Preet Singh?"

"Yes."

"Yes, I have. Let me try," Mohan started playing the notes.

"Is that okay?" he asked after a while.

"Perfect," I said.

"Okay, guys. So, it is a song from the movie called *Aiyaary*. Let's enjoy the song," Mohan announced.

He played the opening notes on the guitar. I looked at him sideways and sang:

Mainu ishq tera lae dooba

Haan ishq tera lae dooba...

My eyes met Mohan's, and we exchanged smiles.

Tu shamil hai mere, hansne me, rone me

Hai kya koi kami, mere paagal hone me

I glanced at Mohan. I wanted to tell him that it was not just a song I was singing. But it was exactly my situation. I was madly in love.

People applauded as I finished the song. Some of them also came to me and shook my hand in appreciation. I was delighted. And why not? I had expressed my feelings for Mohan in front of everyone, though I didn't know if Mohan had understood me or not.

After the song, the guests proceeded to have dinner. I too ate my food with my sister and Mohan.

"So, from when should I expect you?" Archana asked Mohan as we ate our food.

"Well... from next Monday. What do you say?" he said.

"Perfect," said Archana.

"How about your auditions, Meera?" asked Mohan.

"Guru ji and I are working on a few songs for the audition round," I replied.

"Why aren't you eating something, beta? I can see your plate is empty," Mohan's mother said, coming up to us.

"I am fine, auntie," I said.

"What fine? Eat properly, Meera," Mohan said and took my plate from me. He came back after refilling it.

"How's everyone at home, beta?" auntie asked further.

"Yeah, everyone is fine."

"Why don't you bring your parents here someday?" she said.

"They are quite busy, auntie." I knew they would never come to Mohan's house, which was not even tenth the size of our bungalow.

"Okay, you enjoy. Let me attend to the other guests."

"Don't worry, Ma. I will take care of them," Mohan said to his mother.

"What is that?" he pointed at my face.

"What?" I checked with my fingers.

"I guess, it is some gravy," Mohan said, removing it from just above my lips.

His touch made me blush.

"Thanks," I said.

He smiled.

"The food is delicious. However, I can't see your best friend Nusrat," I said.

He laughed. "She is not in town. She is a good girl by the way."

"Everybody is good, except me," I said.

I can't say about boys, but for us girls, it is impossible to listen to the praise for another girl from one's lover.

Mohan laughed louder. "You are really sweet, Meera."

"Huh," I said, gazing at my plate.

My sister stared at me as Mohan joked with me.

"Water," she said and went away from us. She had sensed that we needed some space.

You should be careful in front of her. She is no longer a kid, I told myself and dug into my gulab-jamun with the spoon.

I looked up at Mohan, who was busy eating his food.

The whole world understands that I am in love with you, Mohan. When will you understand that? I wanted to tell him, but took a deep breath instead and put the sweet into my mouth.

"Have you gone crazy, Meera?"

I heard as I picked up Mohan's call an hour after coming back from his house. I was checking my Instagram when I got his call.

"What happened?" I asked.

"An iPhone?"

"So?"

"I don't need an iPhone, Meera," Mohan said. "And I can't accept such an expensive gift."

"A gift is a gift. But if you don't want to accept it, then throw it away," I huffed.

"Hey, don't be upset, yaar. I don't mean to hurt your feelings. But..."

I shushed him. "Don't look at the price. Consider it only a gift from your..." I paused for a second to search for the right words.

"Best friend," I managed with the words I hated the most, especially when it came to my relationship with Mohan.

"Huh," Mohan took a deep breath and exhaled.

"Did you like it?" I asked.

"Very much," he said.

"The party was good."

"Thanks, Meera. In fact, you were the topic of discussion after your performance. People simply loved you!"

"Really?"

"Yes. My mother was also saying that one day you will become world-famous," Mohan said.

"If she says so, it will definitely happen." I smiled.

"Hmm. So, how are your preparations for your singing competition going?"

"Yes, it is on Sunday. We have selected a few songs for the audition round. I have to choose at least three songs and practice them," I said.

"Superb."

"You have to come with me, Mohan."

"Me? Are you sure?" he said.

"Yes, I need you there."

"But your mom will also be there with you, no?"

"Yeah, she will, but just before going for the audition, I would like to see you."

"What if your mother sees me there?"

"Then tell her that you have also come for the audition. You anyway sing, don't' you?" I suggested.

"I do, but only for fun. I am not participating in the competition."

"That only you and I know."

"Hmm," he said. "Okay. See you on that day."

"Why? We are not meeting before that?" I asked curiously.

"We can. But how? School's over. I can't come to teach you maths any longer."

"Haha. That's true. But you are coming to teach Archana, aren't you?"

"Yeah, but that's from next Monday," he said.

"Oh, yes. Okay, let me plan something."

"Okay, plan and let me know. But don't plan a visit to Kushmi forest."

I didn't say anything for a few seconds. And then we both burst into laughter.

[12]

"I think *Bairi Piya* would be the best for you," Guru ji said.

We were discussing about the song that I would sing in the audition round.

"But you should be ready with one more song for backup."

"Ji, Guru ji," I said.

"So, let's work on *O mere shona re*. This would be your back up song."

I nodded and decided to sing the song *O mere shona re*, originally sung by Asha Bhosle ji.

"Don't modulate your voice too much. Do it only wherever necessary. For example, don't stretch '*Re*' too much," Guru ji said after I finished the song.

"Ji Guru ji, I got it." I smiled.

"Perfect then. You are ready for the audition. All the best. Don't let me down, my favourite student," Guru ji said, standing up.

I moved forward to touch his feet.

"*Vijayi bhaav*."

"Thank you so much, Guru ji," I said excitedly.

Just a day before the audition round of the singing competition organised by ZH TV channel, I felt a strong desire to meet Mohan and thus called him to Ramgarh Taal. It is a huge lake with a circumference of eighteen kilometres located in Gorakhpur. And trust me, it is the best hangout place for the youth. You can go boating or jet-skiing here, or simply sit at various places around it. The sight is pleasing to the eyes.

Gorakhpur was called Ramgram in the sixth century B.C. And Ramgarh Taal is said to have come into existence because of river Rapti. It's a popular place with tourists.

"Hey, Mohan," I waved my hand as I saw him.

Mohan smiled, waved back and walked towards me. My driver had dropped me five minutes ago.

"What happened? Why did you call me at such short notice?" he asked me.

"Because I wanted to meet you," I said.

"That's fine. But your family doesn't like us meeting outside. Remember, what happened last time?"

"Forget about that," I said as I gazed into his eyes. "Let's go boating," I said.

Mohan thought for a while. "Just two of us," he said, pointing at us.

"Why? You want the entire Gorakhpur to come with us?" I asked, my hands on my hips.

Mohan laughed. "No. But I'm reminded of your father's warning."

Come on, yaar, Mohan. I should be the one hesitating. I am a girl, not you. I thought to myself.

"Will you please come with me? I have already bought the tickets." I pulled him by the hand.

Mohan followed me to the platform from where we had to book a boat.

"Bhaiya, paddle boat," I said to the person who collected the tickets from the customers and gave out the boats.

That person helped us get into a boat and gave it a little push into the lake. We started paddling it towards the middle of the lake.

"I thought you would have been practicing for tomorrow," Mohan said after a while.

"I have done. Now, I need some quality time," I said, taking a sideways glance at him.

"I see. So, which song are you going to sing?"

"*Bairi Piya* from Devdas."

"Wow, that's a really nice song."

"It indeed is. I love the chemistry between Shah Rukh and Aishwarya in this song."

"You're right. So, who are the judges on the show?" he asked.

"Most likely, it is Shan sir, Himesh sir, Sunidhi ma'am and Neetu Mohan ma'am."

"Wow. It's going to be a grand show judged by superstar singers."

"Absolutely. I am glad my favourite Shan sir will be present."

We had come quite far into the lake.

"Let's go there," demanded an excited Mohan.

"There is such a crowd. Let's go that side," I said and pointed to a fairly secluded area.

Mohan frowned at me with a smile. "Okay."

The sun was moving down fast. The sky had turned orange and flocks of birds were flying from one end of the sky to another in joy. The sound of their chirping had its own music. We had come to the end of the lake where very few boats were present. Mohan's proximity was continuously intoxicating me. My eyes were heavy and breath fast. I wanted to hold Mohan's hand, but hesitated. He sensed the awkward silence.

"Are you okay, Meera?"

I nodded, looking into his eyes. My legs stopped paddling and lips trembled. I had no idea what I was up to. I only felt that if I didn't express my feelings, I'd burst like a balloon filled with water.

With quivering lips, I spoke, "I am in love with you, Mohan."

"W...w...what?" It was clear he couldn't believe what he had heard. He smiled faintly. "What?"

I took his hand in mine. "I can't hide my feelings anymore. I love you, Mohan."

"Meera. I can understand, but..."

"But what?"

"See, I understand your feelings and I respect them too. But this relationship... is not possible," he said.

Now, it was time for me to get a shock. I didn't expect such a response from him.

"Why?" I said, my voice a little loud. My grip loosened on his hand, and it slipped away.

"Meera, this is not the right place to discuss this."

"Then which place is? Let's go there," I said in exasperation.

"Look. There is a huge difference between the societies we belong to. There is no match. There can never be a match. We can never be together."

"What difference, Mohan? I love you. I don't know about you. But if we both love each other, then there is no difference. If we get along well, that is the ultimate match."

I glared at him angrily.

"You're right, but it doesn't happen so easily in real life. Our families are never going to accept our relationship."

"Screw the families. You tell me whether you love me or not," I said, my heart sinking.

"It's not just about me loving you, Meera."

Both of us had stopped paddling our boat by now. It was floating around freely.

"Then what is it about, Mohan?"

"Meera, I can't hurt you even in my worst nightmares. But nobody is going to accept this relationship."

My eyes had welled up, despite me trying hard not to cry. Tears started flowing down my cheeks.

“Hey, Meera. Look at me.” Mohan turned my face towards him. I sniffled.

He wiped my tears with his fingers. “You should focus on tomorrow’s audition. This is no time to think about all this. We can discuss it later as well.”

“Please, Mohan.” I shoved his hand away and signalled him not to touch me.

Then after a while, I looked into his eyes, but I couldn’t see any love for me. I was heartbroken. I wanted to be alone. I wished to go back. Mohan had sensed my uneasiness and paddled me back to the boating point. We didn’t talk on the way back. My whole world had come crashing upon me. I still couldn’t digest the fact that Mohan didn’t love me. I wanted to cry my heart out.

[13]

A steady chirping of birds woke me up. I had gone straight to bed after reaching home the previous evening. Crying like a baby, I don't remember when I had fallen into a deep slumber. I looked for my phone around my pillow, my eyes still closed. I opened my left eye to look at the mobile screen. It was switched off. I tossed it back on the bed. I stretched my arms and came out to the balcony of my room. The sun had not come out yet, but its orange rays had covered the sky in front of me. My empty stomach rumbled.

"Ranjan bhaiya, tea please," I called out. My head hurt. "And something to eat too."

When I saw myself in the bathroom mirror, I realised I had not changed. I was still in my kurti and jeans. I came back to the room and changed to a loose t-shirt and shorts. Then, I brushed my teeth and came back to the balcony.

Ranjan bhaiya came up with a cup of tea and poha. And biscuits too.

"Thank you, Ranjan bhaiya." I smiled, looking at him.

He smiled in return. "All the best, didi. You have your audition today, no?"

I nodded. "Thank you."

I finished my breakfast and went to take a shower. I had to reach the sets of ZH channel at 8 a.m.

*

There was a huge crowd in front of the sets of the 'The Young Voice of India', organised by ZH channel. I had come with my mother and elder brother Akhilesh. He is five years elder to me, and more like a second father to me. He was in the last year of his LLB. I always avoid going out with him, but couldn't do so this time. My father had asked him to come with me.

I was low on energy, disheartened, and discouraged after the previous day's disaster. I had ten missed calls from Mohan after I had returned home, but I had not attended to any of them.

I was missing Mohan terribly though, and I didn't know if he would come to support me or not.

Anyway, after some time, Akhilesh bhaiya brought the candidate form for me. I filled it and gave it back to him. There must have been more than a thousand people. A phone call startled me out of my reverie.

"Ji, Guru ji," I said.

"Where are you, Meera?" he said. "I am waiting near stall number fifteen with the other students. Could you come here, please?"

"Ji, Guru ji," I said. "Which stall did you say?" It was difficult to hear anything properly amid the clamour.

"Fifteen," he said.

"Okay. I am coming there."

After Akhilesh bhaiya came back, we walked to the stall. There I saw my Guru ji with his other students. They were super excited. And why shouldn't they be? It was a great occasion for aspiring singers. Unfortunately, my excitement was lost, and I had only myself to blame. I had chosen the wrong day for the expression of my love.

"Hey, Meera. Why do you look so sad?" Guru ji asked.

I faked a smile, "It's just the nervousness, I guess."

"Don't say that, Meera. If you become nervous, what will the other students do?" Guru ji said.

"Guru ji always talks about you. In fact, he praises you so much that we are rather jealous of you," one girl said and laughed. All the other students joined her.

"Hey, nothing like that. It's just Guru ji's love for me," I said.

"No, you are really good. I have heard you sing many times," another student said.

"So is everyone else." I smiled. "All the best, guys."

"You too, Meera."

As we finished, Guru ji addressed everyone. "Listen, all of you. The key to your selection will be your confidence. You all are so good that if you don't get nervous on stage and follow what I have told you, nothing can stop you from being selected. I want you all to have a ticket each to Mumbai. Alright?"

"Yes, Guru ji," everyone exclaimed in unison and touched his feet one by one.

I checked my slip. My serial number was 165. Two hours had passed by and the LED screen showed that candidate number 140 was inside. A first round of screening was complete. There was a big screen just outside the main gate of the auditorium, and many small screens put up around the area. The families and friends waiting outside could see how their candidates were performing.

I was sipping my coke, standing under a tree, when I saw Mohan at a distance. My eyes popped out in surprise. I had not expected him to come after what had happened between us. I couldn't react. I looked around me. Ma was sitting on a chair, whereas Akhilesh bhaiya was talking to someone on his phone. Mohan had recognised both of them and thus remained standing at that spot.

He smiled at me. I kept looking into his eyes without acknowledging his smile. I was really angry with him. For the first time, ever since our friendship had started, I had never felt so distant from him. He felt like a stranger to me.

He mouthed 'sorry'. A tear rolled down my cheeks. He gestured that he wanted to talk to me. I shook my head in denial, my eyes moist.

He held his ears, and I couldn't help but smile. All my anger melted away. Now, *I* wanted to meet him.

"I will be back," I said to my mother.

"Where are you going?" she asked.

"To the washroom," I replied.

Akhilesh bhaiya glanced at me, still talking on the phone.

I walked towards the washroom area. It was behind the main set, and therefore, once I was there, I was out of my family's sight.

My heart was beating fast. The equation between Mohan and me was not like before. Now I could not pretend to be his best friend. He knew about my feelings. How could we be just friends?

And there he was.

"I am sorry, Meera. I shouldn't have behaved like that," Mohan started the conversation.

I crossed my hands across my chest and looked away.

"You are looking gorgeous, by the way," he continued.

I was sporting a mustard-yellow georgette gown.

"Thank you," I replied.

"Will you continue to be angry with me?" he asked.

I didn't say a word.

"Okay, we can argue after today's audition round. But, please don't go in this sullen mood, Meera. It will affect your singing."

I looked at Mohan. So, he wanted to lift my mood only because he didn't want me to fail in the audition. Did nothing else matter to him?

"So, that's why you have come here? Out of sympathy?" I glared at him.

"You are again getting me wrong, Meera. Please don't do so. I request you."

"And I request you to go from here, Mohan."

"Come on, Meera. Cheer up!" He kept his hand on my shoulder.

I gently removed it. "Let me be direct with you."

"Sure."

"Do you love me, Mohan?" I asked, my eyes locked with his.

"Is it necessary to ask this question now?"

"Yes. It is absolutely necessary. And it is a simple question. If you do, say yes; otherwise, say no."

Mohan looked away for a while and looked back at me. "I told you there is no future for us."

"Stop it! Just stop it, Mohan!" I cried and started walking back.

"Meera..." Mohan called out, but couldn't stop me. I was reduced to tears.

[14]

"*Meera Singh Rajpoot! Candidate number 165.*"

My name was announced twice. Akhilesh bhaiya's voice drew me out of my thoughts. "All the best, Meera," he said with a thumbs up.

"Thank you," I replied.

How will I perform in this mood? I thought to myself.

I touched Ma's feet. She blessed me, keeping her hand on my head. I then headed to the main gate of the auditorium. I was received by Siddhant Bhanushali and Priya Saxena, who were hosting the show. They asked me to introduce myself on the camera and asked a few simple questions. They were doing this to encourage every candidate just before they faced the audition. Three more candidates were waiting to perform before me. I was asked to write down the details of the song I was going to sing, before my turn came.

I walked into the auditorium with a cordless mike. I must say the ambience was welcoming, with warm yellow and red colours. Four plush chairs stood opposite the dais where I stood. The four judges sat in those chairs, but the chairs were turned around, and they couldn't see me. This is why it was called the Blind Audition Round. I liked the idea, because, in this way, it was only the candidate's voice that judges could focus on. The candidates were given a maximum of three and a half minutes and one paragraph to sing. The judges were free to press the buzzer at any moment during the song. The pressing of the buzzer meant that the judge wanted that candidate in his or her team. If only one judge pressed the buzzer, the candidate would go into his or her team. But if more than one judges pressed the buzzer, the candidate could choose the team he or she wanted to be a part of. If none of the judges pressed the buzzer, it meant the candidate had not been selected.

The judges chattered among themselves for some time, and then asked the musicians to play the song I was to sing. They followed the instructions and started playing the opening notes. I took a few deep breaths and counted in my head: *Ten, nine, eight, seven, six, five, four, three, two, one, go....*

Ye main hun ya koi aur hai meri tarah...
Kaise hua, kaise hua,
tu itna jaruri kaise hua

I was so overwhelmed with emotions while singing the song that tears welled up in my eyes. Mohan was all over my thoughts. Yes, I had changed the song. I was supposed to sing *Bairi Piya,* but I had listened to my heart. I wasn't concerned about being selected at this point. I just sang the song I wanted to.

I had goosebumps by the time the song finally ended. I opened my eyes and saw all the four judges' chairs had turned towards me. It meant all of them had pressed their buzzers. They were all smiling.

"Hey, how beautiful you are!" Sunidhi ma'am spoke the first amongst them. "What is your name? And where are you from?"

"Thank you, ma'am," I said. "I am Meera Singh Rajpoot. I am from Gorakhpur."

"That's cool, Meera. First of all, I would like to ask you why you chose this song. This song has been sung in a male voice. The lyrics are also written accordingly. But you not only modified the lyrics to suit you, but also sung it so beautifully."

I didn't know what to reply. It was unplanned, fuelled only by my emotions.

"Well, ma'am, I just listened to my heart. Someone had once told me that I should only focus on what I am supposed to do and not on the results," I said.

"Wow, that's said by Lord Krishna."

Yes, Mohan told me that. I thought and nodded.

"You must have prepared this song well," Shan sir said next.

"Well, I had prepared well," I said. In fact, I lied, because I had never sung this song before.

"Your voice is magical, Meera. I can see a potential winner in you," said Himesh sir.

"Thank you very much, sir," I replied.

"The best thing about your singing is that you felt every emotion in the song. I can even notice your moist eyes. It was, without doubt, a daring move to sing such a song, that too in the audition round, but you pulled it off well. So, congratulations, Meera," said Neetu ma'am.

"Thank you, ma'am."

"So, now, since all the four judges have decided to take you in their teams, the decision is left to you. Which team do you want to be in?" Himesh sir asked.

My decision had already been made. I thought for a while, and then took Shan sir's name. All other judges acted in funny ways to express their disappointment. I laughed for the first time since I had arrived there.

"Thank you so much, Meera. I need a singer like you in my team. And it is my pleasure that you chose me. I would love to train you," Shan sir said with his charismatic smile.

He came up to the stage and hugged me. Now, I was a very happy girl as he put a lanyard holding his team's card around my neck.

"Thank you very much, sir," I said.

"Welcome to 'The Young Voice of India'."

[15]

I let out a deep sigh as I came out of the auditorium. Ma and Akhilesh bhaiya came towards me. Happiness was written all over their faces. I rushed to them and hugged them. Since the audition was being shown live outside the auditorium on screens, Ma and Bhaiya knew that I had been selected. Strangers came up and congratulated me as well.

"You were just phenomenal, Meera," Bhaiya said as the people dispersed.

"Thank you, Bhaiya."

"She is my talented daughter," Ma said proudly.

"Every mother thinks like that, Ma," I laughed.

"I don't know about others. But I certainly do."

"So, are you done for the day?" Bhaiya asked.

"I don't know. I need to ask for further details," I said.

Just then one person came to me and said, "Meera Singh Rajpoot?"

"Yes." I nodded.

"Please come with me. You need to attend a session to discuss what comes next."

He took me to a room where a team of three people sat. They asked me to take a seat opposite them. One of them asked for my personal information and filled a form. Another person explained the process thereafter. I had to visit their studio in Mumbai after twenty days, when the actual show would start. I was listening to the person, but all I could think about was Mohan.

Was he still there? Did he see my performance? Does he really not love me?

"Do you have any questions, Meera?" asked another person in the team.

I came out of my thoughts and shook my head. "No."

"Okay. If you have any queries in the future, you may contact us on this number. Your ticket and accommodation details will be emailed to you."

"Thank you very much, sir," I said.

"If everything is done, can we leave now?" asked Akhilesh bhaiya.

"Yeah..." I said reluctantly.

Has Mohan already left? Has he become so heartless that he didn't even wait to see my performance? Even if he doesn't love me, he is still my friend. He could have waited till my performance was over.

Meanwhile my mother stood up. She started walking ahead with Akhilesh bhaiya. I darted a quick glance around me. I didn't see Mohan anywhere. Akhilesh bhaiya looked back at me and gestured to me to follow him.

I pursed my lips and nodded.

After walking around hundred meters, we reached the car parking area where our car was parked. Bhaiya sat in the front passenger seat after helping Ma get into the back seat. I sat beside her.

Tak tak.

Someone's knock at my side window startled me. A boy stood there. I rolled down the glass of my window.

"Many congratulations for your selection, ma'am. This is for you."

He handed me a bouquet and sprinted back without waiting for my reply.

"Who is he?" asked my brother immediately.

"I don't know," I said, taking a look at the beautiful flowers. The fragrance of the flowers filled my heart, and a smile spread over my lips.

Wait! There was a message card stuck in the bouquet. I quietly took it out and stole a glance at my brother. He was looking straight as the driver had started driving the car.

Could you come behind the Apple advertising stall? Someone is waiting for you.

My heart started racing.

"Stop, stop, stop!" I babbled.

"What happened?" bhaiya asked.

"I forgot one of my acknowledgement slips there in the meeting room." I couldn't make up a better excuse.

The driver stopped the car.

"Go get it fast," Bhaiya said.

"Sure, just give me ten minutes." I got down, leaving the bouquet behind and quickly walked towards the stall which was near the main entrance of the auditorium.

[16]

I looked around me, my hands on my hips. There was nobody behind the Apple advertising stall. The temporary stall had been set up in front of a two-storeyed building, the main door of which was locked.

Who has called me here? I wondered, suddenly a bit nervous. *Is it Mohan or somebody else? What if it is somebody else?*

For a moment, I felt scared. However, I plucked up my courage and went near the building. Just then I felt something brush past my hand. I stopped dead in my tracks. It was a piece of paper folded into two. It fell on the ground. Before I could bend down to pick it up, another folded slip fell on my head. Soon it started raining folded slips of paper. I was stumped. I extended my hands, trying to catch some of the slips.

In few seconds, there were a bunch of slips scattered on the ground around me. Surprised as well as excited, I picked up a few of them. I looked around me, and then towards the building roof from where the slips had been falling. I couldn't see anyone. I quickly unfolded one slip. It read –

I love you too, Meera

My heart jumped out of my chest. And my right hand automatically went over it, probably to make sure my heart was there in its place. My happiness knew no bounds.

Where the hell are you, Mohan? Where are you, the man of my dreams? I wanted to scream. But I couldn't. I knew he was there and I looked around desperately for him. My heart was beating fast. And just then I saw him appearing on the roof above me. He was smiling. The most charming smile I had ever seen in my life. And all of a sudden, tears started streaming down my cheeks.

He got down with the help of a pipe, and within seconds, he stood before me.

He waggled his eye brows. "What happened, Miss Meera Singh Rajpoot?"

"Words fail me to describe how mean you are," I said with trembling lips.

He wiped my tears with his thumb. "Should I help you?"

I looked into his eyes and suddenly clung to him. I embraced him tightly. He caressed my back.

"Couldn't you say this before the audition? Was all this necessary?" I said, still hiding my face in his chest.

He laughed. "Trust me, I didn't plan anything. I just couldn't see you in pain anymore."

I moved back immediately. "What do you mean? Are you doing all this out of sympathy?"

"No, no. Absolutely, no." He gazed into my eyes. "I love you, Meera. I can't hide my feelings anymore."

"I love you too, Mohan. And I can't imagine my life without you." I nudged his nose with mine. We exchanged smiles.

Just then a loud noise of applause startled us. Were those claps for us? But there was nobody around us. I then realised that some singer had most probably been selected.

"Now go. Bhaiya and auntie would be waiting for you," Mohan said to me.

I nodded. “Thank you, thank you, thank you,” I was smiling ear to ear.

“There is no need to thank me. I love you too,” Mohan said.

“Bye, I will call you as soon as I reach home.” I was super excited.

“Sure.”

“I am keeping some of them,” I said and collected a few slips. “Could you give me the remaining ones later.”

“Why?”

“They are special to me. Please,” I said childishly.

“Okay.”

“Thank you,” I said while walking back. I held those slips tightly inside my fist and rushed to my car. It had taken much longer than ten minutes.

[17]

The very next day, we were sitting in Brewerz Coffee Bar in the Park Street area of Gorakhpur. I was sipping my cold coffee with my eyes locked with Mohan's.

"What happened?" He arched his eyebrows.

I finished my sip. "I am over the moon."

My smile wasn't ready to leave my face that day.

He brushed the hair on my forehead. "We have a long way to go."

"I know. The journey is not going to be easy."

"Therefore, before I ask for your hand from your parents, I need to become something."

"That's true. What have you planned, Mohan?"

"The plan is the same. You already know what I want to become."

"An IAS officer?"

He nodded. "But you know? The percentage of success in this toughest exam in India is less than one percent."

"Whatever! I know you will clear it."

Mohan smiled and sipped on his cold coffee.

"Have you decided what you want to become?" he asked.

"Yeah. I want to become a professional singer," I said. "And that's why I am planning to pursue a BA course in philosophy."

"What is the connection between singing and philosophy?"

"There is no connection. I just want to do an easy course," I grinned.

"I am sure you will be a famous singer one day."

"And you will be an IAS officer." I blinked my eyes. "A nice combination, no? An IAS officer and a singer."

I picked one French fry and took a bite of it.

"Not bad," Mohan laughed. "We'll register in the same college. While we graduate, I shall also prepare for my IAS exam."

"Yes," I said. "And Mohan..."

"Yes?" He looked up at me.

"I want you to be there on the finale day of 'The Young Voice of India'."

"But how? It would take place in Mumbai, no?" he asked.

"Don't worry. I will send you the flight tickets and will book a hotel in Mumbai."

"But Meera, your family will be there. What if they see me?"

"You love me, right?" I asked.

"Of course."

"*To jab pyar kiya...*" I winked at him, "*to darna kya*!"

Mohan smiled. "That's true. *Jab pyar kiya to darna kya!*"

[18]

Two days before The Young Voice of India, Finale

"Sir, I want to sing some other song in the finale," I said to Shan sir.

We were there in Shan sir's cabin. I had qualified for the finale with three more candidates: Abhijeet Mukharjee, Anjali Deshmukh and Vineet Jha. After several rounds of screening, we had secured the finale spot out of twenty-four candidates who had participated in the show. All my performances had been loved by the judges as well as the audience. Now, it was very difficult to say who would be the winner in the end. The stage was set for the finale. Our families had reached Mumbai. Akhilesh bhaiya, my younger sister Archana and my mother were staying in Hyatt hotel. It was two kilometres away from our shooting set. My mother had been with me all these two months, whereas Bhaiya and my sister had come specially for the finale. Papa, as usual, didn't have time. I had sent flight tickets to Mohan, and he was arriving a day before the finale. I had booked a room for him in another hotel which was about three kilometres from our shooting set.

"Which song?" Shan sir asked. He stood behind his chair with his arms on top of its back.

"*Jab pyar kiya to darna kya*, from 'Mughal-E-Azam'," I said.

I wanted to sing this song because I wanted to tell the world about my feelings. And it would be specially dedicated to Mohan, who would be sitting in the studio on the finale day. I could not think of a better song.

Shan sir smiled. “Any specific reason for this song?”

I hesitated, wondering whether I should tell him the real reason or not.

“Any problem, Meera?” asked Shan sir.

“No, sir.”

“You can share with me. I am asking because this song is not an easy song. And the problem is if someone doesn’t sing it with emotion, it will leave no impact on the audience,” he said. “In my eyes, you have the maximum chances of winning this competition. I don’t want you to make a mistake at this point and lose.”

“I understand, sir,” I thought for a while. “Can we do a rehearsal?”

“Certainly, we will. But before that I have to know the reason for your selection of this song.”

I had got to know Shan sir to some extent in these two months. I could trust him. And that’s why I decided to tell him.

“I am in love, sir,” I said.

Shan sir smiled. “I see. Interesting, Meera! And that’s why you want to sing this song and tell the world about your love.”

I nodded with smile.

“So, who is he? One of the contestants?”

I shook my head in denial.

“Then?”

“He is from my hometown, Gorakhpur. His name is Mohan.”

“Mohan! Nice name. And nice match. Meera... Mohan,” Shan sir said.

“Thank you, sir.”

“Okay. So, will he be there in the finale?”

“Yes, sir.”

"Okay, I won't be a villain in your love story. Let's rehearse."

And for the rest of the day, I practiced the song with him. In the beginning, he wasn't happy with my singing. But after several attempts, I got it right to a good extent.

"Give your hundred percent, Meera. Even a small mistake can take the trophy away from you. Anjali is going to give you tough competition. So, be careful," Shan sir said.

"Don't worry, sir. The trophy will be ours."

"All the best, Meera." Shan sir kept his hand on my head.

[19]

A day later, just before the finale, Mohan had landed in Mumbai around 3 p.m. I couldn't wait to see him. I first decided to go to Hyatt and meet my family, and then to Novotel, where Mohan was staying, to meet him.

I stayed with my family in the hotel until 4 p.m.

"I am leaving, Ma," I said.

"Okay. Let me come drop you," Akhilesh bhaiya offered.

"No, no, why? I will go myself. I have been commuting alone for these two months," I said.

"That's fine. But now, since I am here, I can't let you go alone," Bhaiya said.

"You are worrying unnecessarily, Bhaiya. Rest and just be with Ma. I will go," I said.

"*Arrey*, I am coming with you."

My head spun. *How would I stop Bhaiya from coming with me? How could I tell him that I was going to meet Mohan?*

I tried one more time. "Bhaiya, your dear sister has grown up. She doesn't need your protection anymore."

I smiled to make him not feel offended by what I had just said.

"Do you see, Ma, how grown-up your daughter has become!"

"Come on, Akhilesh. She is right. You don't need to be over protective. She will go," Ma said to him.

"See," I pointed at Ma, looking at Bhaiya.

"Let's go sightseeing, Bhaiya," Archana, my sister also helped me by diverting the topic.

"Yes. That's what you should be doing in Mumbai," I said and picked up my sling bag. "Bye. Enjoy Mumbai, guys." And I left the room.

I rang the doorbell. "May I come in?"

I moved the door handle down, and the door opened. It wasn't locked from inside.

"Hey, Meera." Mohan had recognised my voice.

As I pushed the door open, I saw him in front of me, smiling. I sprinted and clung to him.

"Hey, what happened?" he asked, caressing my back.

"I am seeing you after fifty-eight days, seventeen hours, thirty-four minutes and twenty seconds. Don't say anything. Just be like this." I pressed myself warmly towards him with my arms around his neck and eyes closed, as my heartbeat upped. We remained still for quite some time.

Finally, I leaned back to face him. My smile knew no bounds and so did Mohan's.

"How are you?" he asked.

"How can I be without you?" I replied.

"It's not good to allow someone to affect you so badly."

I pretended to look at him angrily with my lips clasped and eyebrows narrowed. "It's also not good to steal someone's heart so badly."

Mohan laughed.

"Coffee?" he asked.

"Yep." I nodded.

He called from the intercom and placed the order for two cups of coffee and chilli cheese toast. We came and sat beside each other on the sofa in the room.

"So, ready for the finale?" Mohan went to the window and pulled open the curtains. The room was on the seventh floor. The crowded city view welcomed us.

"Yes," I said.

"All your performances were just wonderful. However, I loved '*Tum jo aaye, zindagi me, baat ban gayi*' the most."

"Yeah, because it is true, no?" I beamed.

Mohan touched my forehead naughtily.

"There is something on your eyelids, Meera. Let's me remove it, otherwise, it may go inside your eye," he said.

"Okay," I said, trying to look at my own eyelids.

Mohan came close and blew air gently over my eyes. Just then a loud voice startled us.

"*What the hell are you doing to my sister?*"

I looked towards the door where the voice had come from. It was Akhilesh bhaiya! I couldn't believe he was there, inside the room. He must have followed me!

"Bhaiya... Bhaiya... listen to me," I said, standing in between Mohan and him.

"You step aside, Meera. I am out of my mind! How dare this rascal touch my sister?" Bhaiya roared.

"Nothing like that! You are mistaken, Bhaiya," I exclaimed. "By the way, what are you doing here?"

"What am I doing here? My own sister is asking me this question?" Bhaiya's eyes were red. "You tell me what are you doing here?"

"That's none of your business, Bhaiya. I have my own life. It's between me and him. I request that you stay out of it, please."

"Bhaiya, what you're thinking is not true. I was just..."

Before Mohan could complete his sentence, Bhaiya slapped him hard, pushing me aside.

I was stunned. The slap hurt my soul. I hadn't expected such a reaction from my elder brother.

A few seconds of silence occupied the room. Mohan didn't say a word as Bhaiya kept staring at him.

"You shouldn't have done that, Bhaiya," I broke the silence.

"Now, will you teach me what I should do?"

"I request that you leave us alone." I didn't make eye contact with him, pointing a finger at the door.

"What is going on between you guys? What is he doing here in Mumbai? And what are you doing in his room, Meera?" Bhaiya fired a series of questions at me, glaring at Mohan all the while.

"Bhaiya, I will answer all of your questions. But not now. You are not in the right frame of mind at the moment," I said.

"I see. Okay. I am leaving, but you're coming with me," he said.

"No. I am not."

"Then you have to pay for what you are doing, Meera."

"I am ready," I said angrily, still not looking at him.

Bhaiya kicked the centre table and left the room.

I looked at Mohan. He smiled. Tears appeared in my eyes.

"I am so sorry, Mohan," I said.

He kept a finger on my lips and gestured not to say anything.

"How did Bhaiya came here?" I murmured to myself. "I should have been more careful."

"Whatever! The point is, now your family knows about us. Let's discuss how we will put up our defence," said Mohan.

For the next half an hour, we discussed about how we would defend ourselves when the news would reach my parents.

What a terrible evening it turned out to be, just before the finale! Now the song that I was going to sing in the finale truly suited my situation.

Pyar kia koi chori nahi ki...
Chhup chhup aanhen bharna kya
Jab pyar kia to darna kya...

[20]

The stage was set. It was decorated beautifully. My turn was second after Vineet. I had chosen a white coloured kurti with a yellow salwar. The dupatta was also yellow. I looked at the audience towards my left. Mohan was sitting there. The hard slap had left a black spot under his left eye. I was deeply hurt. I turned my gaze and looked towards my right and in the audience were my mother, sister and Akhilesh bhaiya. I tried to smile at my mother and sister, but gave a stern look to bhaiya. Finally, my eyes stopped at Shan sir. With both his thumbs up, he wished me luck. I smiled in response and mouthed 'thank you'.

The musicians started playing the song. *Four, three, two, one, zero....*

Insan kisi se duniya me
Ek baar mohabbat karta hai
Is dard ko lekar jeeta hai
Is dard ko lekar marta hai
Pyar kiya to darna kya....

As the song ended, the auditorium reverberated with the sound of applause. However, my eyes were locked with those of Mohan.

After all the performances were done, we were called up on stage. All the judges were also there. Hosts entertained the audience before handing the mic over to the judges. Each of the judges gave their remarks on the performer. Shan sir announced the performer in the fourth position.

"Although it's really difficult to say who is the best singer at this stage, yet due to the format of the show, we have to choose one winner. It is time to announce the performer who is at the fourth spot."

A timer started. Its sound made everyone's heartbeat go up, including mine. After a little bit of drama, he called out, "Vineet Jha."

I let out a big sigh of relief.

Abhijeet Mukharjee came third. So the winner was either Anjali Deshmukh or I. Sunidhi ma'am was to announce the winner. She took Anjali and me to the centre of the stage. I stood on her left. She held our hands. The timer began once again as Sunidhi ma'am looked at us successively.

"What's going on in your heads, girls?" she asked with a smile.

"Nothing actually! Excitement has overwhelmed me," said Anjali.

"How about you, Meera?" ma'am looked towards me.

"Whosoever wins, I will be happy," I said.

"Okay, so, the wait is over, audience. I know you guys can't hold your nerves anymore. So, the winner of The Young Voice of India is..." Sunidhi ma'am paused. But the timer continued.

I closed my eyes.

"The winner tonight is..."

The audience roared.

"And the winner is..."

I felt my hand being lifted by Sunidhi ma'am. I had won! I opened my eyes as the public chanted my name – '*Meera, Meera*'.

I couldn't hold back my tears. My eyes stopped at Mohan. He stood up at his place, super excited, clapping hard, with an ear-to-ear smile on his face. I rivetted my gaze at my mother and sister. They were smiling and clapping for me as well.

For the next few minutes, nobody spoke. All I could hear was the sound of applause. It was a double dose of happiness for me. Earlier, I had received Mohan's acceptance of my love. Now, I had the trophy as well.

I was surrounded by so many people. Everyone wanted to congratulate me, shake hands with me. But I only wanted Mohan.

"Please allow him to come," I told the people around me as I saw Mohan trying to inch his way towards me. People understood he was special to me and made way for him. I wanted to see him smile. And he did. Wow, that smile! I just can't describe in words what it did to me. I couldn't practice any restraint and just hugged him. The people around us cheered and clapped. I knew my family was there, and they must have certainly not liked it, but I was in love and didn't give a damn.

"Hey, Meera, control your emotions," Mohan said.

"I can't express how happy I am in this moment. Let me enjoy the feeling, Mohan."

"Is he your boyfriend?" someone in the crowd asked.

I didn't say anything. I simply smiled.

"Tell us his name at least, ma'am," said someone else.

I released Mohan and faced the public.

"He is Mohan," I replied.

"Is he your boyfriend?"

"Everything doesn't need to be said, sir," I said with a smile.

"Absolutely! Can we have selfies with you, ma'am?"

"Of course," I said and posed with people.

"This way, Meera ji," someone said.

I looked towards the other person's camera and smiled. The selfie session went on for almost half an hour. I looked for my family, but didn't find them. A storm was about to be unleashed, and I started mentally preparing myself for it.

[21]

The show was over. My family took me back to Gorakhpur the same evening. They didn't allow me to attend the success party for all the contestants. It had been scheduled for the next day. Bhaiya had told Papa everything and asked him to call me back immediately. Papa spoke to me over the phone and ordered me to obey bhaiya. I didn't want to go completely against my family, especially my father. If I wanted to marry Mohan, I needed my father's support. Thus, I left for Gorakhpur with my family.

The next day, Papa summoned Mohan and me to his office. We stood opposite him. He was seated in his chair, his right foot over his left. I looked at him. He was smoking his cigarette. Smoke and an awkward silence filled the room. Neither Mohan nor I dared to initiate a conversation. It was better to wait for Papa to finish his smoke.

"Is what I have heard from Akhilesh true?" Papa finally broke the ice, rubbing his cigarette butt in an ash tray kept on the table in front of him.

"I don't know what Akhilesh bhaiya has told you," I replied.

"Then you tell me what's going on between you guys?"

I searched for the right words. But, if you are in love, what could be the right words! *So, how should I tell my father? Should I directly tell him that I was in love? Doesn't it sound weird? So, what should I say, "I like Mohan"? Or, should I say, "we are just friends."? I think to lie is not a good option. The opportunity has automatically come to us. We can admit the truth now and then see what happens next.*

"I am talking to you, Meera," Papa interrupted my chain of thoughts.

"Yeah," I stuttered. "Papa, we are in love," I said.

Papa let out a deep breath and narrowed his gaze at us.

"What is love?" he asked.

His question shocked me. *So, do I need to explain to him what is love?* I wondered. *So, he wants to see what I understand by love. I should give him such a definition that impresses him. What should I tell him? What should...*

"Okay. I like his nature. Our thinking matches. We really get along well with each other. And if I speak my heart out, I want to marry him and spend my whole life with him," I finished my definition of love.

"Do you also have anything to say?" Papa asked Mohan.

"I have similar feelings for her," Mohan replied.

Papa took another cigarette from the packet and lit it.

"You guys are too young to think about all this. This is your age to study and think about your career, and not to fall in love," Papa said and took a drag of his cigarette.

"You are absolutely right, Papa. We don't want to marry now. We want to make something of ourselves. I want to become a singer, a professional one, like the ones who sing for Bollywood movies. And winning this show has opened the door for me, Papa. Similarly, Mohan also wants to become a Civil Services officer."

"Yes, sir. In fact, I have started preparing for it," Mohan added.

"Listen, I don't want to go into debate mode. I just want to tell you guys that this relationship is not possible," Papa said.

"But why, Papa?" I asked immediately.

"Don't misunderstand me. And also, I am not looking down upon you, Mohan. But there is a huge gap between my family's status and yours. And I don't see this gap being filled anytime soon. I love my family and social status both. And thus, I can't allow this relationship to materialise in the future," Papa concluded.

"Please, Papa. Don't be like that stereotypical father of Bollywood. I know you are so modern in your outlook. What is the problem if Mohan becomes an IAS officer a few years later?"

"It is not just about a position. They are Yadavs, and we are Kshatriyas. This relationship is not possible." Papa took another puff.

"Papa, please. This is the twenty-first century. Caste and creed don't make sense nowadays. Humans have landed on the moon. How can we still be talking about caste?"

"Look, you guys are still in school. You haven't seen the real world. That is why you talk like this," Papa said.

"We will be in college in a month," I said.

Papa gazed into my eyes, took a deep breath and said, "One last time, I am telling both of you. This relationship will never be possible. It's better that both of you focus on your career and families. There is nothing more important than family. I hope it is clear to both of you. Now, you may leave. And not only this, you will also not study in the same college."

I was surprised. Was my father giving me a warning?

"Sir, please don't punish us so for loving each other," Mohan said.

I stood paralysed. Tears welled up in my eyes.

"Is that clear to you guys?" Papa ashed his cigarette in the ash-tray.

"No, sir," said Mohan.

I looked at him, surprised. Was he going to revolt then and there only?

"What do you mean by 'no'?" Papa asked him.

"Sir, this has happened in the past also."

"What?"

"The more lovers are forced to stay away, the closer they get. The more efforts that are made to break their bonding, the stronger it gets. By doing so, you are only bringing us closer," Mohan said.

"So, what do you suggest? Should I give my daughter's hand to you myself?" Papa said, getting a little worked up.

"That's the best choice," Mohan said.

Papa had been very patient so far, unlike his nature. But Mohan's retort had irked him. He stood up and came close to us.

He slapped Mohan.

I was shocked.

"Don't you dare talk to me like that again!" Papa pointed a finger at him, his face red.

"Don't consider someone's respect for you his weakness, sir. I request you not to hit me again," Mohan said.

I burst into tears. My family wasn't treating Mohan well at all. Immediately, I caught his hand and walked towards the door. After walking a few steps, I turned back and said to my father in my broken voice, "I didn't expect such behaviour from you."

"I too didn't expect this from you, Meera," Papa said out loud. "But remember, as long as, I am alive, I will not allow anyone to tamper with me and my family's respect."

I was seriously upset, and Papa's words only provoked me further.

"And as long as, I am alive, I will not leave Mohan," I replied to Papa.

"I knew this was going to happen, Meera. Your family is never going to accept our relationship," Mohan said, disappointed.

We sat on a rock in the vicinity of Ramgarh Taal. I clutched Mohan's hand and looked into his eyes.

"I am with you, no matter whether my family accepts us or not."

Mohan kept looking into my eyes. "I know, Meera. But this love is only going to cause us pain. Nothing else."

"Then I am ready for the pain. I can live with this pain. But I can't live without you."

I noticed a teardrop rolling down Mohan's left eye.

"I am not going anywhere. Don't worry," I said, my face hid in his chest.

He patted me on the back.

After some time, we parted and faced each other. Our eyes were locked. It was a magical moment. Suddenly, Mohan moved closer to me and kissed me on my cheek. I wasn't expecting a kiss at that moment. A ripple of joy ran through me. It was a sublime feeling indeed.

"What?" Mohan asked mischievously.

I shook my head.

"So, why are you smiling?"

"What was that, Mohan?"

"What?"

"That one." I pointed at my cheek.

"What? I don't see anything there."

"Mohan!" I raised my eyebrows.

"Okay, if you insist, let me check if anything is there." He brushed his fingers on my cheek, moving closer to me.

I tried to look into his eyes, but he was too close to be seen. Before I could understand anything, he kissed me again.

"Mohan!" I exclaimed with joy and mock-punched him. He embraced me as the cool evening breeze blew past us.

[22]

Two Months later

"What is this?" I asked as Akhilesh bhaiya dumped a booklet on the dining table in front of me.

My entire family was at the table for dinner.

"Your admission form," bhaiya replied while sitting on his chair on the other side of my father.

"Which college's admission form?"

"M.D. College."

"I told you I want admission in D.N.P.G. College," I said.

"Papa has decided that you should go to M.D. College. You just need to fill the form. Your admission will be done."

"And may I know which course you have chosen for me?" I crossed my hands across my chest.

"Which other course? B.Sc. only," Bhaiya said.

"Do I have any right on my own life or not?" I asked exasperatedly. "I am neither going to study B.Sc. nor in M.D. College."

"Meera! Is this how you talk to your elders?" my mother shushed me.

"Ma, is this how my elders should interfere in my life? Let me be clear about this. I want to study philosophy in D.N.P.G. College."

"Philosophy?" Papa looked at me, surprised.

"Yes, philosophy."

"Philosophy is for those who can't study anything else. And what career options are there in philosophy?"

"A career in singing. And philosophy I want to study because I am interested in it."

"Your daughter has gone mad," Papa said to my mother.

"Why don't you listen to you father, Meera?" Ma said to me.

"Ma, please, try to understand me."

"Okay. That's your choice. But make sure that guy doesn't study in the same college as yours," Papa said.

"Come on, Papa! Don't stoop to this level and drag my studies into all this."

"Shut up, Meera! Don't talk to Papa like that," bhaiya said.

Papa interrupted him. "Let her speak. Otherwise, she will complain that we don't allow her to speak also."

"Papa, please. At least, let me choose what I want to study and where," I requested.

He looked at me for a while and then said, "Okay. You decide where and what you want to study. I will decide where and to whom you will be married."

"Now, what is that, Papa?"

"Look, Meera. I am giving you a choice. You can decide and let me know. No more discussions. The food is getting cold," Papa said and tore a piece of roti on his plate.

Everyone focused on the food after Papa put an end on the discussion. He started discussing work with Akhilesh bhaiya.

"Can you pass me the rice?" I said to my sister.

She stared at me and put the rice bowl in front of me with a thud.

Why is she angry with me? Is it because I am revolting against my family? I wondered and served myself some rice. *But she should be happy. If I succeed in marrying according to my own choice, it will also open the door for her.*

I stared back at her and arched my eyebrows asking her what had happened.

She shook her head and looked down at her plate as if saying – *What'll happen if you fail, Meera? Would it not close the door for me as well?*

[23]

Three Years Later

We were graduates now. Three years had passed by in the blink of an eye. These were probably the best three years of my life. Mohan and I studied in the same college. We went for college outings, partied and spent some really good times. But soon, it came to an end. Our final year exams were over. Mohan had planned to move to Prayagraj for his preparation. I decided to pursue my post-graduation from the same college.

It was the month of May. One fine evening, my father called me to his room.

"Yes, Papa," I said.

He was doing some work on his laptop. Upon seeing me, he took off his spectacles and kept the laptop aside. He signaled me to take a seat. I obeyed him and sat on the sofa next to him.

"How are you?" he asked.

"I am fine, Papa," I said and thought. *What is he up to? Please don't bring up anything related to marriage.*

"Now, since you have done your graduation, it's time you should be settled."

"As in?" My brows narrowed. There is only one meaning of 'being settled' in our country.

"I have selected some highly qualified and good-looking boys for you. Let's start meeting them."

"But Papa, I am not ready for marriage. I am just twenty-two."

"That is the best age to get married. Your mother was only nineteen when she got married."

"Please don't compare Ma's life with mine, Papa. Nana wasn't as educated as you are," I said.

Papa shot daggers at me and took a deep breath. "Listen, Meera. I agreed to your demand of studying the course of your choice as well as the college. Now, it is your time to fulfil my demand."

How do I tell Papa that I love Mohan, and I can't imagine a life without him, I thought. *No matter what, you can't give in to Papa's demands, Meera.* I told myself.

"Papa, you know I can't marry anyone else."

"Shut up, Meera! Just shut up! Don't bring up that issue again!" Papa yelled at me. "You will marry who I will choose for you."

"No, Papa!" I opposed.

"Meera!" Papa yelled and slapped me hard.

Ma came running into the room as I covered my cheek with my right hand.

"What happened?" she asked worriedly.

"Ask your daughter," Papa continued yelling. "I want to secure her future. And she is determined to humiliate me. That boy is still on her mind."

I gazed at the floor and dug my toes into it, my hand still on my cheek. For the first time in my life, I had experienced a slap. It not only hurts you physically, but also your self-esteem.

"What's happening to you, Meera?" Ma came to me and shook me.

I looked up into her eyes. I felt broken, yet I collected myself and said, "I won't marry anyone other than Mohan."

Ma kept her hand on her mouth. "Are you shameless, Meera? How could you even talk like this in front of your parents!"

I didn't respond. I wanted to get away from there.

"Listen, Meera. You are no longer a kid, so don't behave like one. Nobody understands better than us about what is good and what is bad for you. So, let us fulfil our responsibilities towards you."

"I know I am no longer a kid, and that's why I am behaving like an adult. Even the Constitution of India says that an adult has the right to make a choice about his or her partner."

"I don't need to learn what the Constitution says from you, Meera. Mr Rana Chauhan's family is coming tomorrow to see you. So, make up your mind, and don't create a scene tomorrow. Otherwise, you will see the worst side of me."

"You can't force marriage on me, Papa," I said in a shaky yet firm voice.

"I don't want to force anything on you, Meera. But you're not giving me an option. Take your daughter from here. I have a hell lot of work to do," Papa said to Ma in anger.

Ma tugged at my hand. But I shrugged her off and stood up myself. I shot an angry look at them and left the room.

I fell face down on my bed and cried loudly, clenching the pillow against my face.

What do I do now? Should I elope with Mohan? Would Mohan agree? What if these Chauhans approve of me as their future bride? How would I survive even a day without Mohan in my life?

My head was throbbing. I called Mohan.

"Hi, Meera," Mohan said as he received the call.

I broke into tears.

"What happened, Meera? Are you okay?"

I controlled myself and told him about everything that had happened.

"Ohh..."

"What 'oh', Mohan? My family is after me," I said.

"Let me think of something," he said.

"Think whatever you may. But I can't live without you, Mohan."

He thought for a while.

"I think you should meet that guy tomorrow. There is no other way," he suggested.

"What do you mean, Mohan?" I said angrily.

"What else can we do? You meet him and tell him the truth."

"What truth?"

"That you love me and can't marry anyone else."

"And then he will immediately tell his family. And his family will tell mine. And then what, Mohan?" I asked.

"Then we will see what we can do. Look, Meera, we have to show our resistance. It is our fight with our families. The one who breaks down first is the one who loses."

I thought for a while. "Hmm... okay."

"I know it is a long and tough fight. But we have to face it, Meera," Mohan said.

"I understand, Mohan."

"Then smile and stop worrying, sweetheart!"

I smiled and began to feel a tad better.

[24]

The next day, the Chauhans visited our family. I got ready unwillingly. I wore a firozi salwar suit with matching earrings. I kept it simple, yet the Chauhans liked me. They said they were greatly impressed by my simplicity, and I hated them for that. The boy's name was Kuldeep. He was good looking, tall, fair-complexioned, and well-built. He had completed LLB and started his practice under his father's legal company.

After the usual question round that a girl has to go through, Kuldeep's mother said, "Kuldeep beta, if you wish, you can talk to Meera in private. It is important that you both understand each other well before getting married."

My eyes popped and I wondered. *When has the marriage been fixed? Did I say 'yes'? No, I didn't. Why is this lady considering it done? But it is good that she is suggesting that we go talk alone. I need to speak to Kuldeep.*

Kuldeep smiled and looked at me. I felt a little uncomfortable as all eyes were on me.

"Yes, of course," my mother seconded Kuldeep's mother.

"Meera, why don't you show Kuldeep your room?" Papa asked me.

"Sure," I said and stood up. "This way," I gestured at Kuldeep. He smiled and followed me.

After talking a quick round of my room, we stood in my room's balcony. It was evening time and the sky in front of us had turned orange.

"Would you like to have something?" I asked Kuldeep.

"Only if you give me company," he said.

"Some juice?"

"Okay."

I called Ranjan bhaiya and asked him to get us some juice.

"You are beautiful," Kuldeep said.

I didn't like Kuldeep saying that, but I couldn't be rude.

"Thanks," I acknowledged.

"I am told that you're fond of singing. So, you want to become a singer?"

"Yes, I do," I said. "That's the only dream of my life."

"My family doesn't have any problem. We are quite open-minded people."

"I appreciate that."

"In fact, it is good that you can follow your passion sitting at home," Kuldeep said.

"Sitting at home? How?" I wondered out aloud.

"Well, you can practice and sing whenever you feel like."

"I think you don't understand the meaning of a professional singer. I want to sing in Bollywood. For that, I may need to shift to Mumbai as well. Will you and your family be comfortable with that?"

I thought it was better to say things that would disappoint Kuldeep, so that he said 'no' to me himself.

Kuldeep laughed.

"Why are you laughing?" I asked.

"Well, I can understand your feelings, Meera. It is due to your age. As you get mature, you will think differently."

"No, I will not think differently. And if maturity will make me think like that, then I will not become mature."

Kuldeep leaned against the parapet and crossed his hands across his chest, gazing at me.

"I like the way you express yourself," he said.

"I am not kidding, Kuldeep. If I am not allowed to live my dream, I can't marry you," I said. I thought if the differences in our thinking could solve the problem, then I needn't bring Mohan in between. Who knew, Kuldeep himself might reject me after knowing about my aspirations?

"Don't worry. I will help you live your dream," Kuldeep said.

He broke my heart. *Why are you being so nice to me?*

"How about your family? They may have problems with my aspirations," I said.

"To be honest, they may. But don't worry, I will convince them when it is required."

Oh my god! Why Kuldeep why? Why are you ready to compromise so much? You should give more priority to your family. You can't make them angry on my account.

"I don't want to be the cause of any disturbance in your family," I tried another argument.

"Why are you being so negative?" Kuldeep smiled.

Just then Ranjan bhaiya brought a plate with two glasses of fruit juice.

"Thank you," Kuldeep said, picking up one glass and handing me another.

"Thanks," I acknowledged.

He took a sip of his juice. "If we get along well, there is no problem. Trust me."

Should I tell him the truth or should I exercise some more options? But are there more options? I thought.

"Kuldeep, I am really sorry to say, but I can't marry you," I plucked all my courage and said it.

Kuldeep narrowed his gaze at me, rolling the sip of juice in his mouth. "Why?"

"Because I am in love with someone," I finally admitted.

"Then what's the need of all this pretence?" Kuldeep kept his glass on the wall and stood up straight.

"I am sorry. I have already told my family, but nobody is ready to listen to me. You look like a sensible man, so I am telling you."

Kuldeep shook his head in disappointment and started walking away.

"Kuldeep," I said.

He stopped and looked back at me.. "Yes?" he said.

"I am so sorry."

He didn't say a word and walked out of the room.

[25]

The drama had begun in the living room. My father was trying to assure Kuldeep's father that I would act according to him only and that it was childishness. However, Kuldeep's father didn't look convinced. He asked for some time to ponder on all the aspects. All my family members looked worried. I was more worried thinking what would happen to me after Kuldeep's family left.

And eventually, Kuldeep's family took their leave. His father assured Papa that he wasn't rejecting the proposal completely, but he certainly needed time to think about it.

I mouthed 'sorry' to everyone, but I was sure it didn't leave any effect on anyone. Papa came to me and looked at me. I turned my gaze down. I felt like I was a lamb trying to stand upright on its trembling legs before a lion. I remembered Papa's slap. And there he went. He slapped me once again..

"Enough is enough, Meera. You are going to marry none other than Kuldeep."

My nostrils flared. I lost my cool and screamed my head off with my eyes closed, "*I have told you. And I repeat. I will marry only Mohan, nobody else!*"

I received another slap. And this time it was from my mother.

"You've completely lost your mind, Meera. You are becoming shameless!" she said.

"If it is so, disown me," I screamed.

"I wish I could. But we are your parents, not your enemies," Papa said.

"Then behave like them," I countered.

"There is no point in any discussion," Papa said to Ma. "Let me fix the engagement date. You and Akhilesh begin the preparations."

"I will kill myself rather than marry Kuldeep or anyone else," I said loudly.

"Get lost!" Papa said and stormed out of the living room, followed by the others.

I felt so helpless and alone, and clinging to the wall in front of me, I cried my heart out.

*

The same evening, Papa summoned Mohan's father. My younger sister Archana told me later that Papa had reprimanded him severely. He complained about Mohan and said that it was him who had seduced me away from my family. Mohan's father obviously didn't like such allegations against his son. Later in the night, Mohan called me up and informed that his parents were in a state of shock.

"Nothing is in our favour, Meera," said Mohan.

"I know. What to do now?"

"Papa is saying if I don't promise that I would not meet you and talk to you, then he'll go back to our village. He can't afford to fight a lawyer."

"So, what did you say, Mohan?" I asked. For the first time, I could sense defeat in his voice. Was he broken? Was he thinking about leaving me?

"I am with you, Meera. But at the moment, my priority is to protect my family. I can't get them into trouble."

"I understand, Mohan. Even I wouldn't like you to throw them in any kind of danger. But some kind of trouble can't be avoided."

"I agree with you, Meera. Your family has become a bit aggressive."

"I know," I said.

"I am worried, Meera," he said after some moments of silence.

"So am I, Mohan."

"What do we do?"

"Let's get married before my family forces me to marry someone else," I suggested. And I meant it.

"What are you saying, Meera?"

"I am serious, Mohan."

"Are you sure?" he asked.

"Yes."

"You wouldn't back out at the last moment?"

"Where do you want me to meet? Let's get married today itself," I said. I was intoxicated with emotions.

"How would your family react?"

"They would react insanely. But what can they do after that? They are not criminals, Mohan. Over time, they will accept us," I said.

Mohan thought for a while and then said, "I am filled with strength and hope when you talk like this, Meera."

"I love you, Mohan."

"I love you too, Meera."

We decided to marry the very next day. I had taken the biggest decision of my life. I had mixed feelings: fear, excitement, happiness – all at the same time.

[26]

I took my sister Archana in my confidence and told her everything. Her first reaction was like she had touched a high-tension electric line. She was in total shock. She rejected my idea outright and refused to provide any help. Rather, she threatened that she would tell our family about my plan. I had to convince her a lot and give her the assurance that I loved my family too, just like she did. But at that moment, I needed her support because it was about my entire life ahead of me, and nobody in our family was ready to understand me.

Eventually, she agreed. Without her, I couldn't go out of my house, that too so early in the morning. I told Ma that I would be going to the temple with Archana. She was a bit surprised because I had never visited a temple so early in the morning. I loved going to temples, but only in the evenings. But since Archana was with me, Ma didn't give it a second thought.

I got up at four a.m. the next morning. We left home around five and reached the Radha-Krishna temple on the outskirts of Gorakhpur.

It was 6 a.m. My best friends Reena and Disha had also come. Mohan had come with two of his friends. I was clad in a simple green salwar suit. Reena had brought her make-up kit. We went to the back of the temple, where Reena and Disha helped me get ready. My eyes welled up.

"Hey, Meera. What happened?" Reena asked softly.

I just smiled and shook my head.

"Excited, no?" Disha poked me.

I bobbed my head in affirmation.

"Where are you guys going for your honeymoon?" Reena said while covering my head with my dupatta.

"*Dhat!*" I blushed, although the thought overwhelmed me with joy and excitement. "We are too young for a honeymoon."

"Aha! You are not too young for marriage. But you are too young for the honeymoon? Beta, I know you better than Mohan. So, don't lie to me," Disha said mischievously.

"Shut up, yaar! Focus on what you're doing," I said, but couldn't hide my smile.

Disha laughed.

"Now, you look like a bride," Reena said and held her mobile in front of me. "Check out."

The selfie camera was on. I looked myself in the camera. With a dupatta on my head, a large bindi on my forehead and kajal around my eyes, I did look like a bride to be. I applied a red coloured lipstick and took a deep breath.

The sun had started peeking its head above the horizon. The sunrays were making various parts of the temple gleam in a reddish hue. Even though it was May, the mornings were pleasant. The smell of sandalwood *agarbattis* and fresh marigold flowers filled the temple. My heart was beating at the speed of a bullet train.

The two parties stood facing each other with the panditji in the middle. I stood with Archana, Reena and Disha beside me, while Mohan stood with his friends. Mohan had worn a white chikan embroidered kurta with a pair of blue jeans. His wet hair was well combed. Our eyes met and smiles were exchanged. I was hypnotised. I had never thought that I would get married like this.

These things happen in films, Meera. What is all this happening with you? The thought passed through my mind.

I took long deep breaths. Mohan's friends gave one garland to me and another to Mohan. The smell of jasmine flowers made everything ambrosial as I looked into Mohan's eyes.

"You have to go first, Meera," pandit ji said.

"Ji, Panditji," I said and raised my hands towards Mohan. He bowed a little, but the moment I tried to put the garland around his neck, he stood up straight. He laughed with his friends. I raised my brows, and kept my hands on my waist.

"Okay, okay. Here is my head. You can do whatever you want to." Mohan bowed down to me.

I promptly garlanded him. He stood up straight and leaned towards me and put the garland in his hands around my neck. As tears of joy rolled down my cheeks, I noticed Mohan's eyes had also become moist. We hugged each other tightly as our friends cheered and threw flower petals on us.

The rest of the formalities were done soon. Pandit ji recorded our names in a register which he used for registering the names of the people who got married in that temple. He wished us a happy and prosperous life ahead. We entered the temple and took the blessings of the lord.

We were back home by nine a.m. I was over the moon. Life around me seemed different that day. Afterall, I was a married woman!

[27]

In the evening, I was talking to Mohan in my room, when Papa, Ma and Akhilesh bhaiya barged into the room and stood in front of me. My heart came to my mouth. It was not usual. Papa and Akhilesh Bhaiya rarely entered my room.

"I will call you later," I whispered to Mohan and kept my phone aside. I got off my bed. I had an inkling what all this was about. I hadn't thought that they'd come to know so early. I wasn't prepared for it. Was it Archana who couldn't keep my secret?

I glanced at them. Their faces were red with anger.

"*Badtamiz ladki*, you didn't think even once before disgracing us?" Ma grabbed me by the shoulders and shook me. "Because of girls like you, Meera, nobody wants to be a parent of a daughter," she said and gave me a tight slap across my face.

"What have I done that makes you feel ashamed of me?" I yelled.

"*Besharam*, after getting married secretly, you are asking what you have done?" Ma yelled back at me.

" I had no choice because of you. You didn't leave me any option."

Papa came forward and made me sit on the bed.

"Listen, my child, I understand you are in love with that guy. But love is not enough. I will manage everything. You just have to say that you have been forced into this marriage. Please do as I say, Meera, for the sake of our family."

"Papa, I have married Mohan. I can't ditch him." My eyes got teary.

"But you can ditch us?" Papa's eyes broadened.

I shook my head. "No."

"That's what you have done, Meera."

"Please, Papa, try to understand me. Mohan is a gem. If you love me, then you should give my hand to Mohan yourself."

"Shut up! Just shut up, Meera!" He stood up and looked at me.

"Either leave Mohan or leave us," Papa said and walked out of the room. At the door, he turned back and said, "You have only tonight."

And he left after dropping a bombshell. I was rooted to the spot, struck dumb.

What does he mean by saying I only have tonight? Does he mean I have to leave my house if I choose Mohan? Do I mean only this to him? I was broken. I looked at Ma who was bristling with anger.

"I don't think differently from your father," she said and left the room too.

"Now, the respect of the family is in your hands, Meera. Take your decision consciously," Akhilesh bhaiya added before leaving.

I was aghast. *What the hell do I do now?* I wondered. I was absolutely not ready for this. I started feeling cramps in my stomach.

I dialled Mohan's number.

'The number you have dialled is not reachable at the moment. Please try again later,' the computerised voice said. I broke out in cold sweat.

What the hell! Where is Mohan? Why is his number not reachable? Is he in some danger? All kinds of thoughts arose in my mind except that he might have deceived me. I knew anything could happen in the world, apart from Mohan betraying me.

In the next half an hour, I dialed his number approximately fifty times, but in vain.

Something is wrong. Mohan wouldn't keep his phone unreachable without a reason. I told myself. It was 8 p.m. Every passing second was no less than climbing a steep mountain. I decided to go to Mohan's house. When I reached there, I found out that Mohan's family had also learnt about our secret wedding. He had been thrown out of his house. I had expected all this to happen somewhere down the line, but not so soon. We set out with no destination in mind. At 9 in the night, we were on the roads of Gorakhpur. I was thirsty, and Mohan bought a water bottle from a shop and handed it to me. After having a sip of water, I looked into his eyes. He smiled, probably to make me feel better. I realised he was my life at that moment. I clung to him and burst into tears.

"Hey, Meera..." he caressed my back. "Don't worry. It is just a matter of a few days. Then things will be fine."

"We have not done anything wrong, no, Mohan?" I asked.

"Absolutely not!"

"Then why are our families behaving like this. Are we not their kids anymore?" I said hiding my face in his chest, holding onto his t-shirt.

"It's not their fault, Meera. It's our society. What can they do?"

"What do we do now, Mohan? Where do we go?"

"Let me talk to Mama ji. He will certainly show us some way."

Mohan talked to his mama and asked for his help. Mama ji talked to one of his friends and managed to make arrangements for our stay. Mama ji's friend owned a house which he had let out to three tenants. A small room was empty. He suggested we take shelter there for a few days.

We readily agreed.

It was a small room. Mama ji and his friend had come with us. Mama ji had brought along a thin *gadda* and two cotton sheets. He had also brought us some food and two plates. After everyone left, I lay the mattress on the floor and opened the packets of food. There were some chapatis and mixed sabzi. The turmoil of emotions had come to a halt, and I realised how hungry I was. Mohan kept two plates in front of us. I moved one plate away and put all the chapatis and sabzi on the other. Mohan looked at me and smiled. He tore one piece of chapati, wrapped some sabzi in it and extended his arm towards me. I had tears in my eyes as we fed each other.

After having dinner, we lay down. Although, we were married, it was too early for me to accept the fact that I was going to sleep with Mohan. To be honest, I was not comfortable.

What would happen if Mohan tries to get physically close with me? I thought. My mind was flooded with thoughts. I had a habit of sleeping in shorts and a loose t-shirt. The only pair of clothes was the one I had been wearing, a salwar suit.

Summers in Gorakhpur were at its peak, and I was used to sleeping in an air-conditioned room. There was no such luxury now, but I was happy with Mohan. We lay on our sides, facing each other. A constant smile on my face was obvious.

"So, how're you feeling?" asked Mohan.

"Super-duper happy."

"So am I."

Mohan entwined his fingers into mine. He was so close to me, I could smell his breath. Slowly, I lost myself in his beautiful eyes. My heart was beating fast. What was going to happen? I had no idea. I was excited for sure, but at the same time, I didn't want to indulge in a love making session so soon. However, I wanted to be romantic. I kept my foot over Mohan's. He smiled at my move. He kept his right hand on my back and pulled me towards him. Now, our faces were almost touching. I closed my eyes. My lips started quivering as

I could feel the warmth of Mohan's breath on my face. And just then my phone rang.

"Augh!" I grunted and picked it up. "Archana?" I exclaimed.

My heart skipped a beat. *Why is she calling me now?* I thought.

"Hello," I said.

"How are you, di?" she asked me in a tense voice.

"I am fine, sis. How did Papa come to know about all this? Did you...." I asked.

"No, di. I didn't."

"Oh! Okay. Why've you called up?"

"Di, actually, there is bad news," she said rather breathlessly.

"Bad news! What happened?"

"Ma and Papa tried to kill themselves."

I felt like someone had pulled the ground from underneath my feet. I sat up immediately.

"What! What are you saying, Archana? Tell me it's not true"

"I am not lying, di. I am not lying."

"Where are they?"

"They are in hospital, in the ICU," she said in a quivering voice.

"Oh my god! What the hell were they trying to do?" I cried out. "I am coming. Which hospital?"

"Live Life hospital."

I disconnected the call and looked at Mohan.

"Let's go," he said to me and held my hand. I couldn't control myself and broke down. I cried my heart out. I had not thought about such consequences to my actions. My parents had tried to kill themselves as they thought I had sullied their reputation by marrying a boy from another caste!

What if my parents die? Will I ever be able to forgive myself? Is marrying someone you love such a big crime? What would be the meaning of life if my parents are not alive. I don't want a life of my own choice if it takes away my parents. It is better to die than be the cause for your parents' death. In either of the situations, there is no life for me. Why is god taking such a tough test? I kept on thinking on the way to the hospital.

[28]

I ran towards Archana as I saw her in the corridor of the seventh floor of the Live Life hospital. I grabbed her by the arms. "How are they?"

She gazed at me with tear-filled eyes and shook her head. "Still not out of danger."

I moved a step back, my hand over my mouth. My legs turned to jelly and I crumpled into a heap on the floor right there. I kept my head between my knees and cried bitterly. Mohan sat beside me and caressed my head.

"Control yourself, Meera! And have faith in god. They will be fine," he said to me.

"I am so sorry. I am so sorry, Papa and Ma. I feel so guilty, Mohan. My parents are in the ICU because of me," I said with a heavy heart.

Mohan took my hand in his and smiled. "Don't worry. Nothing will happen."

Meanwhile, Akhilesh bhaiya came over to us. I stood up to face him. "What are the doctors saying, bhaiya?" I asked.

He looked away from me, tears in his eyes.

"Bhaiya, please, talk to me," I said.

"Meera, nothing can be said for the next twenty-four hours," Akhilesh bhaiya replied.

"But what did they do to themselves?"

"Doctors are saying they have taken some poisonous drug."

"Poisonous drug!" I exclaimed.

"I want to see them."

Akhilesh Bhaiya game me a stern look as I said that.

"Please." I folded my hands.

"Okay," he said and took me to the ICU.

I saw my parents from a four-square feet glass window outside the ICU. They lay next to each other in their beds. Their faces were covered with oxygen masks. I couldn't bear to see them in such a state and turned away. I was laden with grief and guilt. If this was the consequence of me marrying someone of my own choice, I was not ready to face it. I wanted to run away from everyone, including Mohan. I felt dehydrated and my eyes became heavy. My head spun, and I collapsed.

By the evening, the doctors allowed us to meet my parents. I found it difficult to look into their eyes. I sat on a stool by the side of my father's bed. The moment we saw each other, both of us began to weep. I held his hand.

"Why, Papa?" I asked, my voice choked.

"I wish you a happy life with Mohan," he said in his shaky voice.

"This is how you wish me a happy life, Papa?" I asked. "It is better that you kill me instead."

"How can I? You are my daughter."

I kept my head on his hand and let my tears flow freely.

"You have to promise that you guys won't do such a thing again. Promise me, Papa," I said.

He didn't say anything and looked away from me.

"Papa, I am asking you something," I repeated.

He still remained silent. I shook his hand. He looked at me.

"I am bound by the society rules, beta. I can't help you."

My father's changed tone made me realise how helpless he was feeling.

"I don't need any help, Papa. Just promise me that you'll not harm yourselves," I said.

"I can't make any promise to you, Meera."

He withdrew his hand and again started looking away. Helpless, I went to my mother and held her hand. She closed her eyes.

"Ma, please talk to me," I said.

She didn't speak at all, even after my several attempts to make her.

"At least, open your eyes, Ma. Have I become such a stranger?"

"Beta, don't make them emotional," one of the ICU staff interrupted me. "Try to make them happy, not sad."

I was devastated.

What the hell do I do? How do I make them happy? Should I lie to them that I would leave Mohan for the sake of family's respect. But would that lie help in the long run? Wouldn't that be more harmful when they'd come to know that I had lied. What do I say to them?

I couldn't make a decision and thus stood up to leave. But fear housed in me. If I left without assuring my parents that I wouldn't go against their wishes, then they might not recover soon. This assurance was the need of the hour. But how could I give them this false assurance?

Meanwhile, a doctor entered the ICU along with a few junior doctors. Immediately, he went to my father and started checking his pulse.

"Show me the last vitals," he said to one of the ICU staff. One the them showed him a paper.

"Who is she?" The doctor pointed at me.

"Their daughter," said the staff.

"Don't allow anyone much time. They are still critical," the doctor said.

Those words gave me another shock. "Why are they still critical, doctor?" I asked.

"Because the effect of poison is still not nullified."

"When will it be so?"

"Next eighteen hours are critical," the doctor said. "They need mental support from the entire family. You have to motivate them to live. Keep them happy."

The doctor wrote something on a piece of paper the gave it to the staff. "Add these medicines through IV. And keep me posted."

And the doctor went to the next bed in the ICU.

I had to take a decision. Mohan or my parents? I loved Mohan and living without him wasn't possible for me. But I couldn't live with the burden of guilt if something happened to my parents. I went straight to my father and said to him. "Don't worry, Papa. I will do what you want me to. If you ask me to leave Mohan, I will ..." I couldn't complete my sentence and ran out of the ICU.

Mohan stood waiting for me.

"What happened, Meera? Are you okay?" he asked as he saw me.

I couldn't dare to look into his eyes.

"Are uncle and auntie fine?" he asked.

I looked up into his eyes and shook my head. My lips were trembling and I felt so weak and helpless. Had I ditched Mohan? I had no answers to any of my questions. I wished mother earth would crack and then take me in, just like she had done to Ma Sita.

[29]

Neither Mohan nor I had slept that night. We went to Ramgarh Taal to get some fresh air instead. We sat on one of the stairs that went down to the lake. The cool wind touching the lake water blew past us. I felt a little relaxed and grabbed Mohan's hand firmly. He probably sensed something.

"Are you hiding something from me, Meera?" he asked.

I shook my head unconvincingly.

"But my heart says that you are," he said.

I looked at him sideways. A gust of wind blew some of his hair onto his forehead. "Papa and Ma tried to kill themselves. This fact is killing me now."

"I can understand, Meera. This is shocking. Your father never appeared to be such a weak man."

"I guess I have made them weak," I said.

"Such things are bound to happen, Meera. But when two people are in love, things slowly settle down."

"What if something happens to them, Mohan?"

"Nothing will happen," he said and kissed my hand.

We kept on watching the waves on the surface of the lake as dawn broke, bringing cool air and some light. The birds started chirping. Everything was so fresh, except my mind.

"Can we live with our families for a few days, Mohan?" I broke the silence.

Mohan turned his head to look at me. He thought for a while before speaking. "But our families have shown us the door."

"Yeah, but my family needs me at the moment, Mohan. Don't misunderstand me. It is just for a while. When things fall back in place, I will come back to you." I took his hand between mine.

"What are you thinking, Meera? Tell me clearly," he said.

"I am worried about my parents, sweetheart, and want to spend a few days with them. We are married forever, so don't worry."

"Okay," said Mohan and continued to look straight ahead.

In the afternoon, my parents were shifted to a private ward. I was sitting near Ma. She had not yet spoken to me.

I gave her some fruit juice and she took it without looking at me.

"Ma, please talk to me. You have not said a word to me. Please say whatever you want to. If you want to slap me, please do so. But don't ignore me."

"What is the point?" Finally, Ma broke her silence.

I sat straight up in my chair. "Why do you think so?"

"Because that is the truth. If you listened to us, you would not have married behind our backs."

"But I did so because I didn't have a choice, Ma."

"So, why are you here? You've married the man you've chosen yourself. Now, let us live however we wish to," she said and sipped some juice.

"But, Ma, you and Papa tried to take your lives."

"And we'll do this again."

"What nonsense, Ma. Please don't say that again."

"Why not? If you are not ready to change your decision, why should we?"

I looked into her eyes. I didn't want to argue with her.

"Leave us alone. Why are you wasting your time here? Your husband must be waiting for you."

My eyes welled up with tears. I couldn't bear such harsh words from my mother.

"What do you want from me?" I dared to ask her, although, I knew I wasn't strong enough to fulfil her desires.

"Just let it be, Meera. I don't want to be dishonored."

My family was playing with my emotions. It was clear. My mother was trying to break me down.

I knew if I allowed my mother to voice her wish, she would definitely ask me to break up with Mohan. But breaking up was not an option for me. I had married him. Thus, I stood up and left the room.

"Don't show me your face ever again." I heard my mother say as I left.

*

Two days later

The discharge formalities were done. I had decided to stay at home for a few days. I stood facing Mohan outside the hospital.

"Are you okay?" I asked Mohan.

He smiled. "Yeah."

"You trust me, no?"

"I do, Meera."

"Don't forget to call me every hour."

Mohan grinned. He took my hands into his. "You take care of yourself. And if there is any problem, promise you will tell me."

"Of course. Who else will I tell?" I said, "You also promise that you will share everything with me."

He mock-punched my nose. I laughed as he hugged me.

[30]

One week later

“Meera!” Mohan called me, huffing and puffing.

“What happened, Mohan?” I asked, worried.

“Papa hasn’t come home since last night. His phone has also been switched off since noon.”

“What?”

“Yes, Meera. My heart is sinking.”

“When did he last speak to someone in the family?”

“Ma spoke to him last morning.”

“This is worrisome, Mohan,” I said and heard Mohan sobbing. “Hey, sweetheart! Don’t worry. Uncle will be fine,” I tried to console him.

“How can you say that so confidently?”

“Should I talk to Papa about it?” I asked.

“Your father! Hah! I suspect it is your father who has done all this,” Mohan said curtly.

“What! Are you mad?”

“Actually, Meera. The fact that my father is missing is making me crazy.”

“We can lodge a complaint in the police station. Let me come with you,” I said.

“No, that I will do, Meera. Can you request your father to let my father return home if he knows anything about it?”

"Sweetheart, if you want, I will definitely ask Papa, but there is no way he is behind it."

Mohan didn't reply.

"Okay, let me ask Papa right away and call you back," I said and went to Papa's room.

I was upset at Mohan's allegation, but spoke to him directly. He denied his involvement. Meanwhile, Mohan went to the police station and lodged a missing complaint.

The same evening, Mohan's father was found sitting on the railway platform number three. The only clothes he had on was his underwear. He was not in his senses. Mohan got a call from the police. He rushed to the spot and took him home. It was embarrassing for him to see his father in such a condition. Later, he took him to the hospital where he was admitted for a day. The doctors confirmed that something had been given to him that caused him to lose his consciousness. Nothing much could be found out about what had happened with Uncle. But I knew Mohan suspected my family's involvement in it. However, I wasn't sure.

A week later, Mohan told me that he was moving to Prayagraj for his civil services preparation. That had been his plan after graduation. We decided to meet at Ambedkar Park. We were meeting after a week, the longest time in recent times that we had not seen each other.

We met at six in the evening.

"How're uncle and auntie?" I asked him.

"They are fine," Mohan replied.

We sat on the lawn. I had worn a pink colour churidar salwar suit. I had also applied a very small sindoor tika. While leaving home, I had covered it with my hair, but made it visible to Mohan.

"How're things at your home?" he asked.

"People don't talk much to me. Although, Papa is nice to me."

"Hmm. The coming days will be tough for us, Meera. People will try everything to separate us."

"I know, sweetheart!" I said and kept my head on his shoulder and held his hand.

"But things will be fine once I become a Civil Servant."

"That is our biggest hope, sweetheart. Please focus on your studies. And don't worry about me. I will be fine. I will pursue my post-graduation here in Gorakhpur."

"Yes."

Suddenly, I sat up straight and looked at Mohan. "What if I also come with you to Prayagraj?"

"I wish you could. But considering the fact that I don't have any money; it would be impossible for me to bear the living for both of us."

"Is love not enough?" I made puppy eyes.

Mohan smiled at me.

"I mean they say that in the movies. Do they lie?" I said childishly.

Mohan laughed at my expressions. "Let's steal some money from your father's account. Then love would be enough."

"Not a bad idea." I chuckled.

We spent a lovely evening together, and then left, making a promise to each other that no matter what, we would stay united. I used to wear a *maala* that my grandmother had given me once. She was a devotee of Lord Krishna. She had performed a puja few years back and had given the maala to me. She said it would protect me from all kinds of dangers in my life. Now, since Mohan was going away from me, I decided it was my responsibility to protect him. I gave it to him.

[31]

It had been a month since Mohan had gone to Prayagraj. I had noticed that he had started avoiding my calls. Whenever I called him up, he would say that he was busy with his studies. His changed behaviour was disturbing.

I could not focus on anything and decided to pay a visit to Prayagraj without informing him. The next morning, I asked my driver to drive me to Prayagraj, while I told my sister Archana that I was going to one of my friends' house and would be back late.

It is a seven-hour journey from Gorakhpur to Prayagraj. Just an hour before reaching Prayagraj, I called Mohan up and told him that I was coming to meet him. He obviously was surprised, but didn't make any excuse, and asked me to come to Café Coffee Day at Hastings Road.

At three in the afternoon, we were sitting opposite each other. His eyes had developed dark circles around them, thanks to his late night studies.

He smiled, but his smile didn't have the original warmth it used to.

"This is why I had to come," I said.

"Why?" Mohan asked.

"You don't look happy to see me, Mohan."

"Nothing like that, Meera. You are misjudging me."

"Your words and expressions don't match."

"It is truly all studies, Meera. I am sleep-deprived here. Thus, you can't feel the same energy."

"Is that the only reason, sweetheart?" I kept my hands over his, looking into his eyes.

Mohan nodded.

"Let me also come to live with you here. Don't worry, we will manage," I said.

Mohan looked down at the table. He was definitely hiding something from me.

He looked up at me. "I wish we could. I really miss you, Meera."

I could see tears in his eyes.

"Mohan, you are hiding something from me. Please tell me. Your silence is killing me," I said.

"My parents' life has become hell. Papa gets various disturbing calls every day," he said.

"What! From who?"

"Don't know. Papa has filed a complaint, but the police is of no help. How can I study with all this going on?"

I was shocked. Was it my father who was doing this? Who else could it be?

"Who do you think is behind all this?" I asked Mohan.

He looked into my eyes. "I don't know, Meera."

"Do you think it is my father?"

"I can't say. But it could be him."

"This is really strange," I murmured and took a sip of my coffee.

"It is."

"So, what have you thought, Mohan?"

"My mother doesn't talk to me, because she feels I am the reason behind all this. And she is not wrong."

I kept my glass aside. I could not take another sip.

"So, what have you thought, Mohan? Please tell me clearly," I said.

"I haven't thought of anything, Meera. I am only trying to focus on my studies."

"No, Mohan. I can feel something is not right.. Do you want to break up with me?" I asked. "Oh, there cannot be a break up. We need to get divorced. Afterall, we are married, no?"

"Meera, you're getting me wrong. I have not thought of any such option. I have married you. I will not leave you, no matter what," he said.

My anger melted away as he said that. His eyes were truthful.

"But we still have to do something about your parents. Why don't you call them here and live with them?" I suggested him.

"Well, it's not that easy. And you think they will stay with me in these circumstances?"

I nodded.

"They will probably go back to our village." He sipped his drink as he looked at me. "What else can they do?"

I had no answer or suggestion to give. I kept quiet.

Later, we went to the banks of the Ganga for a boat ride. There were several boats on the river. What a beautiful sight it was. And what a beautiful evening it was. I sat with Mohan with our hands clasped, watching the orange sky with thousands of birds going back to their homes. I also wanted to make a home with my love, my heart, my Mohan.

While I was on my way back to Gorakhpur, I got a call from Archana. My heart sank. And I hoped it wasn't any bad news. But it was. Papa was admitted to the hospital again.

I directly reached the hospital around 1.30 a.m. Papa was in the ICU again. The moment my mother saw me, she came to me with folded hands. She was crying bitterly. She literally pleaded with me to save Papa's life. Now, that was enough. The dam of my patience and resilience was broken. My mother was begging me. At that very moment I decided to sacrifice my life for my parents.

"Please, Ma. Don't do this." I grabbed her hands and made her sit on a chair. I kneeled down and said to her, "I am ready to do whatever you want me to."

"Then marry Kuldeep, your father's friend's son," Ma said without wasting a moment.

I closed my eyes and remembered god. I was presented a cup of poison, and was supposed to drink it up all. I was so broken, so fragile that I had no energy left to turn down my mother's demand.

"What are you thinking, Meera?" Ma asked me again.

Few tears rolled down my cheeks and I stood up to walk away.

"What happened?" Ma asked again.

"Start the preparations, Ma," I managed to utter and walked out of the room.

I sat on the floor against the corridor wall and hid my face between my folded knees. I recalled my journey with Mohan. The day I had first seen him. The moment we spoke for the first time. The surprise I had got when I had seen him in my house. The time when he proposed his love to me. The time we spent together. Our first outdoor visit to Kushmi forest. His birthday party, my singing audition, and me winning the trophy. Everything went past my eyes as if it were a movie, and now it was coming to its end – a tragic end! I had given in to my family. I had accepted my defeat and agreed to marry according to my family's wishes. Meera, a married girl, was going to marry again. I knew I was going to commit a sin. I was going to cheat on my beloved Mohan. Death seemed easier to me in those moments. I wished it could have come to me, but I just surrendered myself to my destiny. I accepted it, but I was going crazy. I was losing my consciousness and eventually collapsed on the floor.

[32]

One Month Later

Life had changed. Though I was alive, my soul was dead. I was married to Kuldeep. I hadn't informed Mohan, because I knew if I had discussed with him, I would have never been able to do so. I also knew my Mohan would understand my decision one day. I had done this solely for the sake of my parents. They were eager to die because I had married Mohan. I couldn't live with guilt if something happened to my parents. All the ceremonies of my wedding were completed in just four days. I had switched off my phone, so Mohan had no way to contact me.

The next day after the wedding, I switched on my mobile phone. There were a hundred and three missed calls from Mohan's number. My heart melted out of guilt. I wanted to speak to him, but didn't have enough courage. I selected his number in my contact list a few times, but couldn't press the 'Call' button. Frustrated, I dumped my phone onto the table in my bedroom.

It was 9 p.m. Since I didn't have to go out of my bedroom, I picked one plain saree to wear. Just then my mobile rang. It was Mohan. My heart started beating fast. With shivering hands, I received the call.

"Where are you, Meera?" asked Mohan.

I swallowed a lump in my throat, wondering what to say.

"Meera? What happened?" Mohan asked restlessly.

I still couldn't say anything. I was choked with emotions, my eyes filled with tears.

"Meera! Sweetheart! Are you okay?"

I burst out crying. "I am sorry, *jaan*. I am very-very sorry!"

"Meera... what happened? And where are you?" Mohan stuttered.

I took few deep breaths and told him in my quivering voice everything that had happened in the past four days. He didn't utter a word.

"Mohan. I know I am guilty of breaking your trust. I have not been loyal to you. I have betrayed you, Mohan. I am married to someone else. Now, you can give me any punishment you like," I said.

There was no response from the other side.

"Mohan?" I waited for a few seconds, but there was no response.

"Mohan, your silence is killing me. Say something."

"What can I say?"

I could clearly sense the sadness in his voice.

"I am sorry. I am...I am... really sorry, Mohan."

"I wish you a happy life, Meera."

"Please, don't curse me, Mohan."

"I am not cursing you."

"No, no, Mohan. All the doors of life are closed for me. I don't know how long I'll live."

"Don't say that. Take care, Meera. I am hanging up."

"Mohan, please don't behave like a stranger. I am still the same Meera."

"Really? You think so?"

"Mohan, I beg you of you. I won't be able to live a single day."

"I don't know what to say, Meera," he sniffled.

Tears ran down in a steady stream down my cheeks.

"You focus on your studies, Mohan. I want to see you achieve your dreams," I said, wiping my tears with my thumb.

Just then, there was a knock at the door.

"I will talk to you later, Mohan. There is someone at the door," I said and disconnected the call.

It was Kuldeep. He came inside and smiled at me.

"Everybody is so happy. People can't stop praising you," he said, removing his shirt. He changed to a loose t-shirt and shorts.

He came to me and held me by my arms. "You are happy, no?"

I looked into his eyes and faked a smile. I nodded.

"If you have any problem, don't hesitate to share it with me. Mom can be a little annoying at times, but I guess, it is understandable for her age. Don't get hurt because of her," he said and turned the tv on. He lay down on the sofa

In some time, one of the help brought dinner for us and served it on the centre table. It is a tradition that on the first night of the marriage, couples feed each other. Everything in this marriage was like walking on fire. But what could I do? I had chosen this path myself. Anyway, feeding each other was not a big deal. The biggest problem was physical intimacy with Kuldeep. I wasn't prepared for this. I could not imagine in my dreams to make love to someone other than Mohan. I made the very common excuse that I was having my periods. He was obviously disappointed, but understood the situation and thankfully didn't force himself on me. That's how my wedding night passed.

[33]

Days were slowly passing. I was living like a dead person with no excitement, no aspirations, no expectations from life. Every day, I had to make the same excuse to Kuldeep as he tried to get close to me. But how long can you make this excuse? Five days... six days? After that it doesn't work.

It was the seventh night of our marriage. Kuldeep came into our bedroom, drunk. I got scared as I saw him. I could clearly see the lust in his eyes. He came close to me and kissed me on my lips. I pushed him away.

"What the fuck is this, Meera? I am your husband. And I hope your periods are over now," he said, sounding exasperated. "You might make up a new excuse today, but I am not going to buy it. I will make you mine today."

"Listen, Kuldeep. You are drunk. We can't make out when you're like this," I said.

"Enough is enough, Meera," he said and jumped at me. He caught one corner of the pallu of my saree and pulled it. In a second, my saree was in his hands.

"I will complain to Papa ji, Kuldeep. Just stop this nonsense," I yelled out.

"Go, complain now. But what will you complain about? That your husband wants to make love to you? Huh?" He jumped at me again and clutched me tightly. The next second, he drew the strings of my petticoat, making it fall on the floor. I folded my hands and literally pleaded to him to stop. But he didn't listen to me. I closed my eyes and prayed.

He pushed me down on the bed and undressed. I lay there like a statue with my eyes closed. I accepted that I would have to go through it, so I quit fighting. As I braced myself, two minutes passed, but I didn't feel Kuldeep on top of me. I opened my eyes and was surprised to see that he was lying on the sofa, watching tv.

I felt bad. He was not wrong in his place. It was his right to make love to his wife. How many lives were getting ruined because of me! I picked up my clothes from the floor and wore them again and lay down on one corner of the bed. I respected Kuldeep, who despite being drunk, eventually, stopped himself. I had failed in all roles of life: failed as a daughter, failed as a lover, and now failed as a wife too.

After some time, Kuldeep stood up and wore his shorts. He opened his wardrobe, drew out a whiskey bottle and went out of the room. In some time, he was back with an ice box and a tray filled with a few snacks. He made himself a peg and took a sip of it.

I slowly went to him and stood beside him. He pretended not to notice my presence for some time, but when he couldn't do so, he turned his gaze at me. "Now what?"

"I am sorry!" I said.

He rivetted his gaze.

"I am sorry, Kuldeep," I said again.

He sat up at his place. "It is all because of that boy, right Meera? I thought after you get married to me, you will forget that boy. But you are still..."

"I am sorry."

"What should I do with your sorry? I need love, and I want to make love to my wife. If I can't do so, what is the point of getting married? You tell me." He looked into my eyes.

"Give me some time," I managed to say.

"Take your time and make up your mind quickly. I don't want to jerk off every day with my wife lying beside me. Now switch off the lights, I badly need to wank off."

I did as I was told and went back to bed, though sleep was miles away from me. After some time, I noticed that Kuldeep had fallen asleep on the sofa itself.

I came and lay down on the bed, with Mohan all over my thoughts.

[34]

Two Months Later

It cannot go like this. Everybody's life is getting spoiled. Neither Kuldeep and Mohan, nor I am happy. What is the point of such lives! This is a big mistake you have committed, Meera. You have to fix this. I told myself.

It'd been two months now. I was going crazy. Mohan was in my thoughts every minute. Kuldeep was upset on the other hand. Everyday, he would come into our bedroom, drink until late night and sleep.

Mohan had changed his mobile number. Initially, I used to call him every day, but he would convince me not to do so regularly as it would hamper my marriage. Slowly, he began to avoid my calls, and then one fine day, he changed his number.

It'd been around a month since I had spoken to him. I had lost my patience. I decided to meet him. But for this, I had to go to Prayagraj. One Friday, when Kuldeep left for office, I asked my driver and told my mother-in-law that I was going to see my mom and would be back by late night. She was okay with such visits of mine. I left around 9 a.m.

I stopped at Mohan's house. His mother opened the door as I rang the doorbell.

"Namaste, auntie," I folded my hands with a smile.

"Namaste," she replied with a frown.

"Auntie, how is Mohan?" I asked.

"Well, he is fine. Why, what happened?" she asked, worried.

"I wouldn't have come here if I had his mobile number. Please give me his number, auntie" I requested.

"Please, come in," Auntie tugged at my hand and pulled me in the house.

"Why do you want his number? You are married, beta," she said.

"I don't have any wrong intentions, auntie. It's just that I have not spoken to him for the past one month."

"But what is the necessity, beta? You have your family now. If anyone comes to know about your visit, we will be in deep trouble. Please excuse us, beta. We have already suffered a lot."

I grabbed her hands. "I am sorry for everything, auntie. Please give me Mohan's number. I will not cause any more trouble to you."

Auntie shook her head.

"Auntie, please."

"I am sorry." Auntie looked away from me.

Dejected and disheartened, I understood that I was not going to get any information about Mohan from her. There was no point in asking for his address in Prayagraj. I leaned forward to touch her feet, but she stepped back.

Heartbroken, with tears in my eyes, I left. I called up a few of Mohan's friends, but none of them had his number. It seemed to me as if Mohan was punishing me for what I had done to him. I had no idea what to do. How would I search for him in Prayagraj? But my urge to see him was so strong that I commanded Rakesh to drive to Prayagraj. I was not going back without meeting him.

Who can give me Mohan's number? Even his good friends don't have it. Or maybe they do, but *they don't want to share it with me. Has Mohan asked them not to do so?*

Mama ji! Yes, Mohan's mama ji can help me. He had helped us when everyone had rejected us. I asked Rakesh to take the car to the same building where Mohan and I had taken shelter after getting married.

Thankfully, I got Mama ji's friend's mobile number from the tenants living there. And from him, I got Mama ji's number. Immediately, I called him up.

"Yeah, who is this?"

"Mama ji, this is Meera."

"Meera Singh Rajpoot?"

"Ji, Mama ji," I replied.

"Yes, beta. Tell me."

"Mama ji, I want Mohan's number. Please don't say no," I pleaded.

"I am sorry, beta. I can't do this."

"But why, Mama ji?"

"Because Mohan won't like this," Mama ji said.

"I know I am guilty. But please don't punish me," I sobbed.

"I am not punishing you, beta. Please try to understand."

"I am going crazy, Mama ji. If I don't talk to him today, I will do something to myself for sure."

There was silence. I was getting mad at Mohan as well. Why had he decided not to talk to me? Was our relationship so shallow?

"Okay, I will give you his number, but only after talking to him," Mama ji broke his silence.

"No, no no," I interrupted. "If you ask him, he may still refuse. Please, Mama ji, you know how much we love each other. Please do me this favour."

"If you love Mohan so much, why did you marry somebody else?" Mama ji asked.

I knew this was the biggest concern for Mohan's relatives. And I didn't think they were wrong. I was guilty in their eyes. In their eyes, I had deceived Mohan. But nobody knew my pain.

"That I cannot explain on the call, Mama ji. Please give me Mohan's number."

"I am sorry, beta. I can't do that," Mama ji denied flatly and disconnected the call.

I lost my temper. Clenching my teeth, I dialled his number once again. And he disconnected the call.

I started typing a message – *Mama ji, I am requesting you to give me Mohan's number. Please do me this favour. Otherwise, it wouldn't look good if I have to file a false FIR against you for a false allegation. Please call me immediately.*

I felt horrible after sending this message to Mama ji, someone who had helped us when Mohan and I had got married. Situations were forcing me to be a person I was not.

The next minute, I got a call from Mama ji.

"Note down his number," he said gruffly.

Without saying anything, I dialled the number as Mama ji said it out.

"Thank you, Mama ji. And please don't tell Mohan that you have shared his number with me," I said.

"Don't call me up again," Mama ji said before hanging up.

I took a sigh of relief. I finally had Mohan's number.

He may make some excuse if I tell him that I am coming to meet him. It is better to reach Prayagraj first and then inform him, I thought and kept my mobile back.

Around 4 p.m. I arrived in Prayagraj and called him.

He didn't receive my call at first. But he did after two complete rings. I didn't say anything and waited for him to speak first.

"Hello, Meera?" he said.

"Yeah, unfortunately, Meera this side."

"How are you?"

"Why are you pretending to be concerned, Mohan?" I had so much to say to him, so much to complain that I felt I'd burst like a balloon.

"I know you are angry."

"Achcha? What else do you know, Mohan?" I asked.

"Meera, what I am doing is for your good only."

"Who authorised you to think about my good. Everyone in this world is just bothered about me. Everyone just wants to play with my life without knowing what I want, as if I am a football. Everyone kicks me the way they want to." I was livid.

"I am sorry, Meera."

"Shut up! Just shut up, Mohan. Don't say a word." I wiped a tiny tear drop from my left eye. "One fine day, you decided that you should not talk to Meera. And why should you? She is now someone else's wife. But let me tell you, Mohan. First, I am your wife. You could have at least discussed it with me. Simply changing your number and asking everyone not to share it with me is not fair. I can live away from you, Mohan, but I can't live without you in my life. At least talk to me once in a week."

"It is just that I don't want to cause any trouble in your life."

"Trouble? What more trouble can you cause than me having to come all the way to Prayagraj."

"What! You are in Prayagraj?" Mohan exclaimed with surprise.

"Yes. Now, don't say that you are not in Prayagraj."

"I won't."

"Good. So, send me your address."

"You want to come to my room?" he asked.

"Are girls not allowed there?"

"Well, nothing like that."

"So, may I come?"

"Yeah, you can..." Mohan stuttered.

"I am waiting for you message then," I said.

"I am sending it right away."

"Can I say something, Mohan?" I asked. My heart started beating fast. I was going to see Mohan after such a long time.

"Yes, Meera."

"I love you, Mohan."

I didn't want to say that, but I was so overwhelmed with emotions that I couldn't stop myself from expressing my feeling.

Without waiting for Mohan's reply, I ended the call.

[35]

It was a small room. Two single beds were placed along the two side walls. Beside them were two study tables with chairs. There were books all around the room, and several sticky notes were pasted on the walls just above the study tables. Various newspaper cuttings were pinned here and there. Maps of India and the world were pasted on all the free space on the walls. There were two extra chairs in the room. Mohan offered one chair to me. We both were emotional seeing each other after ages. Mohan had become thin. He had grown a beard and his eyes were puffy.

"Are you not eating properly?" I began the conversation.

"I am."

I shook my head, disagreeing with him. "You were not so thin."

"It's because of the studies. Don't worry, I am fine."

I nodded. "The beard doesn't suit you."

Mohan didn't say anything, just smiled. "I am sorry. You had to come so far to meet me," he said.

"You should be sorry for not telling me that you don't want to keep any contact or relation with me."

Mohan turned his gaze away.

"And that is why I have come here. Let's be honest to each other and decide what we need to do next," I said.

"Don't you think you should have informed me that you were going to marry Kuldeep?" said Mohan, looking at me.

"I am sorry, sweetheart. I was carried away. I thought if I discussed with you, I would never have been able to marry someone else. And my parents were adamant on taking their lives. What could have I done, Mohan? I know I am the culprit. But the fact is that I can't live without you."

"But this is not possible, Meera. You are someone else's wife. How can we be together now?"

"We have to find some way, sweetheart," I said.

"What way is there, Meera?" Mohan said, disappointed.

"We will discuss that, Mohan."

"Until I clear this UPSC exam, there can be no solution to any problem in our lives."

I thought for a while.

If Mohan becomes a Civil Servant, I could request Kuldeep for a divorce and then we can again be together. Yeah, that is our only hope.

"But what if you don't clear it?" I asked.

"Then we have to accept what god has chosen for us."

I nodded partially.

"Can I have some water?"

"Oh, I am sorry. I haven't offered you any. What an idiot I am!" He said and went outside the room with an empty bottle.

Curiously, I went to Mohan's study table and looked at it. There were books on the Indian economy, Indian polity, civil services mains essays, etc. The table had a drawer too. I pulled it out. I got curious to see a photo frame inside it. I picked it up to see whose photograph it was. I got goosebumps to find that it was none other than me. I was laughing in that picture. I remembered Mohan had captured the moment when we had gone boating in Ramgarh Taal. He had told me a joke and I had laughed my heart out.

So, Mohan still keeps my photograph in his study table's drawer. But he behaves as if he wants to get rid of me, I thought.

My heart melted away. He too loved me so much. But he refrained from expressing his feelings. He knew if he didn't stop talking to me, my married life would get affected severely. But he didn't know that him not talking to me would also affect my life.

"What are you looking at?" Mohan interrupted my thoughts as he came back with some water.

I turned back to look at him and showed him that photograph. "What is this?"

"You don't recognise yourself?" He took the photograph from me and kept it back in the drawer.

"I mean what is it doing in your drawer? You want to go away from me, no?" I deliberately asked questions, the answers to which would be soothing to my ears.

Mohan poured water in a glass and held it out to me. "You know everything very well, Meera. But the reality is harsh. Let's accept our destiny."

"I can't accept this truth, Mohan. Because I have tried my best, but I can't live without you. I agree I made a mistake. But now, I want to correct it."

Mohan gestured at me to drink the water. Probably, he wanted to interrupt the conversation between us.

"Can we go out somewhere?" I asked him.

"I have a class in some time, Meera."

"I have come so far only to spend time with you. And you deem your class more important?" I said, sarcastically. "Okay, you carry on with your class. I am going back to Gorakhpur."

"Where do you want to go?" he asked with a soft smile on his face.

I couldn't help smiling back.

[36]

In some time, we were standing on the banks of river Ganga. Mohan was talking to a boatman for a ride as I wanted to go boating.

"Come," Mohan told me after getting into the boat. It was tied up to a bollard using thick mooring lines made of ropes that prevented its forward movement.

I stepped down to hold Mohan's hand while holding my saree with my other hand. Something happened as my skin touched his. He pulled me into the boat.

"Thanks," I said and looked around the boat to find a place to sit.

"Please sit on the left side, ma'am," the boatman said to me.

I sat beside Mohan on the front corner of the boat. The boatman began rowing it. The sun was about to set and the fading sunrays reflected off the waves created on the river surface.

"Take us to that side, bhaiya," I said to the boatman, pointing at the other side of the river.

We were looking straight. A strong urge to hold Mohan's hand arose in me. Slowly, I moved my hand over his and entwined my fingers with his.

Mohan turned his gaze at me, pursing his lips, indicating he didn't like my move.

"I am untouched," I said, staring at the horizon taking my hand back.

"Hey, I didn't mean that, Meera," Mohan said and took my hand between his.

I looked at him. Tear drops had accumulated in my eyes. "I had never thought life would be so harsh to me," I said.

"They say, when there is too much darkness, it means dawn is about to break," he said, brushing the back of my hand.

"I will be waiting for your selection in the UPSC."

"I am trying my best, Meera."

"Once you become an officer, I will ask Kuldeep for a divorce. Then, you will marry me once again, no, Mohan?" I asked.

Mohan gazed at me. His expressions said that he didn't have an answer. It disappointed me.

"That depends on many things, Meera. First of all, Kuldeep and his family should be ready for a divorce. Then how your family would react. After all, all this mess has happened because of them only, hasn't it?"

"Why do you always think negatively, Mohan?" I scoffed, drawing back my hand.

"I don't, Meera. I am just trying not to be over-optimistic."

"Huh!" I exclaimed and turned my eyes away from him.

"I am sorry, Meera."

I turned to look at him. "Do you love me? Just answer me," I said.

"What kind of question is this, Meera?" Mohan said.

"Just answer."

"As if you don't know."

"I knew it earlier, but now I am not sure." I became insistent on getting the answer to my question. It wasn't my fault. Even the least dramatic girls act girlish at times.

Mohan happened to smile. "Why do you want to see beautiful dreams again, Meera? And show me the same as well."

"Because to wish for your dreams to materialise, first you have to see them."

"We saw a dream earlier as well, and look where it ended. I am not saying that we shouldn't think of good things. But let's be a little realistic too."

My eyes were glued to his face. I couldn't see the familiar spark in his eyes. He smiled miserably. I was already sad, and Mohan's responses were no respite to my wounded heart. Anger was building up within me. I stood up.

"Meera, what are you doing?" Mohan said anxiously.

"Didi, please sit down. The boat will lose its balance," the boatman also cautioned me, but I didn't pay any heed.

"Meera!" Mohan called me again.

I looked at him sideways. "Do you love me?"

"Stop kidding, Meera, and sit down," he said.

I took a deep breath and jumped into the river.

"*Meera!*"

I heard Mohan scream. I didn't know how to swim, and therefore began to sink into the water. My breathing became irregular, and my lungs sucked in some water as well. Some of the water also went into my nose and I experienced a sharp pain in my head. My hands started moving up and down in an attempt to take myself over the surface. Bobbing in and out, I screamed for help. I could hear frantic voices.

[37]

I threw up more water as Mohan performed CPR on me. I was regaining consciousness. A blurry image of Mohan under the dark sky was appearing before my eyes. I coughed frantically as water came out of my mouth.

Evenings in October are relatively cold in Uttar Pradesh. In my wet saree, I started shivering. It took me half an hour to become somewhat normal. We were back on the shore. The boatman went on complaining all the way back in his muffled voice. He said if Mohan hadn't saved me and I drowned, he would have been in big trouble. He charged Mohan five hundred rupees extra to hush up the matter.

Half an hour passed, and Mohan took me to his room. His landlord asked him who I was. He said I was his cousin and was sick as his landlord gazed at me suspiciously. Mohan walked me to his room on the first floor before his landlord could ask more questions. His roommate was sitting at his study table and studying. I went and lay down on Mohan's bed.

Mohan went to his roommate and whispered something in his ear. He closed his book and left the room.

Mohan pulled a chair and sat near me. I glanced at him. He had a serious face. I had never seen him like that before. Nobody uttered a word for few seconds.

"What the hell was that, Meera?" he asked finally.

I didn't utter a word.

"You jumped into the river, just because you thought I have moved on, and I don't love you." He stood up at his place. "I didn't want to do this. But now you see."

He bent down and pulled out a bag from under the bed.. He then opened the bag and drew out an object that looked like a book. He kept it on the bed in front of me. Then he crossed his arms and said to me, "Have a look."

I sat up and opened it. It was an album. Oh my god! The first picture on it was from the annual function of our school where I was singing on the stage. The next picture was from Mohan's birthday when I had sung a song. I kept on turning the pages of the album, and tears kept rolling down my cheeks. I had never seen most of the pictures myself. The last picture was from our wedding in the temple. It was of the moment I was trying to put the garland around his neck, and he had moved away from me. A big laugh, showing his beautiful teeth took my breath away. Everyone in that picture was laughing except me. I burst into tears as I kept the album aside.

"Now, look at my books," Mohan said further. "It is your name on the first page of each of my books." And he showed me many of his books.

My lips were quivering, head aching, nose running, and throat itching. I was speechless. I rested my head against his and grabbed his shoulders. He sat on his knees before me. I wept like a child.

"I am sorry, jaan. I am sorry..." That's all I could say.

"Just wait for the right time. If god wishes, we will be together, Meera," Mohan said.

I nodded and kissed him on the forehead.

[38]

"I am feeling cold, Mohan," I said as Mohan rearranged his books.

"Oh, yes. You are drenched," he said, looking at me sideways.

He came to me. "What do I do? I don't have girls' clothes."

I smiled at him. "Obviously. Why would you?"

"Should I buy some?" he asked hesitatingly.

My eyes fell upon the clock that sat on Mohan's table. It was six forty-five. I had a seven-hour drive back to Gorakhpur. After so many days,I had got hold of Mohan that I didn't want to leave him so easily. But I had to return to Gorakhpur the same night.

"Meera... what should I get for you?"

"Well, just a saree will do. But where would you get it from?"

"I will buy it. There are a few shops nearby," Mohan said.

"Are you sure?"

"Yeah, of course, Meera," he said, frowning at me.

Mohan pointed a finger at me with a smile. I held my ears in response. He laughed and went out of the room.

I was alone in the room. It had become unbearable to wear those wet clothes even for a second longer. I opened one wooden almirah on Mohan's side of the room to check out some of his clothes. There were not many. I picked one loose t-shirt and a pair of Bermuda shorts and changed. I turned the fan on and put my blouse underneath it to dry it. I sat on the bed with the album looking at our memories again.

[39]

"Hey... you look nice in this attire," Mohan said as I opened the door for him. Half an hour later, he came back with a carry bag in his left hand.

"Really?" I laughed and immediately closed the door behind him.

"Why are you closing the door?" he asked.

"What would your friend think if he comes and sees me in your shorts?"

"Oh, yes." He kept the carry bag on the table. "Here is your saree. I hope you like it."

"Let me see." I took out the saree in my hand. It was yellow saree with pink abstract prints.

"How is it?" Mohan asked.

"Your choice has always been excellent," I said, looking at him, smiling.

Mohan laughed after a while. Probably, he understood what I meant.

"Where is the bathroom?" I asked.

"It is outside."

"So, where do I change?"

"Change here," he said.

"Okay. You go out then," I said.

"I am not going anywhere," he said and lay down on the bed, keeping his hands under his head.

"What!" I exclaimed with surprise and excitement.

"Don't worry, I will turn my face towards the wall. Okay?" he said. I could see mischief in his eyes.

"Promise that you won't look at me," I said to him. To be honest, I was hoping he would. After all, he was my husband.

"Okay, fine," said Mohan.

"What fine! Say you promise."

"I said it, no?"

"When? You didn't say the word 'promise'. Come on, Mohan, say, 'I promise that I won't look at you.'"

Mohan got up slightly and rested his head against one hand with his elbow on the bed. "Okay, I promise. Now, please change." He turned on his side to gaze at the wall.

Quickly, I started changing. "Keep looking at the wall. Confirm you're following my instructions."

"Don't worry. I am," said Mohan. "But this is not fair, Meera."

"If you want to see me changing clothes, then get selected in UPSC exam quickly," I said while making pleats.

"Are you done?" Mohan asked.

"Nope... Don't turn around!" I yelled.

[40]

Mohan put some tea leaves and sugar into the pan and pressed a button on the induction.

Just then a phone call distracted me. It was Kuldeep. I got a little scared.

What if he has discovered that I have come to Prayagraj to meet Mohan?

"Yeah, hi, Kuldeep," I said.

"Get ready. I will be home in forty-five minutes. Then we will go to Samir's birthday party."

"Sorry, Kuldeep. I forgot to tell you that I have come to my mother's house and will stay here tonight," I said.

"Okay. No problem. Come with me. I will drop you back at your mother's place. I told you about this party? Have you forgotten?" he said.

"Well..."

"Samir is a very good friend of mine. And he has invited you especially. Now, if you don't go, it will look really bad."

"Well, I am really sorry, Kuldeep. I am not feeling well today," I said.

"Oh, come on, Meera. Don't make excuses."

"I am not making excuses. Trust me."

"What happened to you?" His tone changed a little.

"I have an upset stomach and a little fever as well."

Kuldeep didn't say a word for a while, then said curtly before hanging up. "I hope you are not lying to me."

My mood was spoiled. Keeping the phone aside, I looked at Mohan, who was making tea.

"What happened?" He asked while straining the tea into two cups.

"Nothing, *yaar*!" I explained the entire situation to him.

He came to me and put the tray on the bed. He picked one cup and held it out with its handle towards me.

"Thanks," I said, grabbing the cup by the handle.

"So, what is the plan?" Mohan asked and took a sip of his tea.

"It is seven-thirty now. I have to be back. I have to tell another lie to my mother that I am at a friend's house to celebrate her birthday and will be back late."

"But if Kuldeep calls your family and comes to know that you are at your friend's birthday party, wouldn't Kuldeep realise you lied to him?" Mohan asked.

I nodded and kept my cup down after taking another sip.

"I hope Kuldeep doesn't cross check," I said.

"We can take a chance to mitigate this possibility," he suggested.

"How?"

"Just call Kuldeep up and say that if it is so important, you are ready to go with him. He can come and pick you up. Also, ask him to get some medicines for fever and an upset tummy."

"What are you saying, Mohan? He will turn up," I said.

"I don't think so. Any sensible man would say, 'Just let it be. Take care of your health.'"

"But if he comes to pick me up, he would only end up knowing that I am not there at my house. This will kickstart the search operation for me." I took another sip of my tea. "Not a good idea, Mohan."

"It's my suggestion. Totally up to you to accept or reject it."

I thought about it. Although risky, but if it worked, it would ease the situation.

"I think I should take a chance before he cross-checks with my family," I said.

Mohan gestured at me to proceed.

I began to speak as Kuldeep received my call, "Look, if it is important, let me come with you. Pick me up."

"Are you sure?" he asked.

"Yep. And please buy some medicines for fever and loose motions."

The word 'loose motions' can put anyone's mood off. And this idea worked for me as well.

Kuldeep spoke after few seconds of silence, "No, that's fine. You get well first. We can go to his house later as well."

"Are you sure?" I asked, but feared if he would change his mind.

"Yeah. You take care," he said.

"Thanks, Kuldeep. You too take care."

I ended the call and tossed my mobile into the air and jumped onto Mohan to hug him. He fell back onto the bed.

[41]

"Which married woman parties so late at her friend's house?" Ma yelled at me.

I was having black coffee to keep the sleep away from my eyes. I had come back at four in the morning and had barely slept for three hours. I was sitting in the courtyard where Dadi ma was doing her morning puja in her small temple, and Ma was grating carrots.

"Arrey, Ma, we had met after a long time. Couldn't keep an eye on the time," I said.

"Beta, stay away from these late-night parties. These are not going to help you in any way."

"This doesn't happen often, Ma. But anyway, I will keep this in mind."

"You better do."

I saw Archana, my younger sister, approaching me.

"Hey, Archana. What's up, dear sis?"

"I am good, di. How are you?"

"Not bad!" I smiled.

"When will you be good, my dear sister?" Archana asked.

"After eating the prasad of my lord." Dadi ma came to us and offered us some dry fruits.

"She is my queen." Dadi sat on her comfortable chair, pointing at me.

"Of course, Dadi! How are you?"

"My life is at its last stage. But I must say Krishna is taking the best care of me."

I smiled. "Dadi, your name should have been Meera, since you love Krishna."

"I didn't get this name, and probably that was why I had decided even before you were born that I would name my grandchild 'Meera' if she was a girl. And Krishna listened to my wish."

"You are so sweet, Dadi," I said and kissed her.

But you didn't think, Dadi, that Meera had a tough life. The in-law's family rejected her. Society rejected her. Pretty much the same is happening with me, I thought.

"It's been a long time since I have heard you singing. Sing something in your beautiful voice, my queen," Dadi said.

"Even I haven't sung for a long time."

"Then this is the best time. Sing me one of Meerabai's bhajans."

"Okay, Dadi."

Ae ri prem diwani,
Mera dard na jaane koi.

[42]

The same evening, I went back to my in-law's house. My mother in-law's behaviour was a little different. Did she come to know anything? I remained normal.

"How is your stomach?" she asked me while having her evening tea.

I looked up at her. Did Kuldeep tell her what we had talked about?

"Yeah, it is much better, Mummy ji," I replied.

"You should have gone with Kuldeep yesterday."

"Yes, Mummy ji. I said I would come with him, but he asked me to take rest. He said we could pay a visit to his friend's house later."

"Huh." Mummy ji twisted her lips to a side.

Around nine, everyone had their dinner, and then I went up to my bedroom. Kuldeep followed after twenty minutes.

"So, Meera? How was your trip?" he said, removing his shirt.

I jumped out of my skin. This meant Kuldeep knew. Or was he talking about some other trip. I had to be sure.

"Which trip?" I asked, nervously. My face turned pink. I knew my lies were caught.

He laughed as he hung his shirt on a hanger in his wardrobe. "How innocent you can play, Mrs Meera?"

I knew there was no point in pretending.

"It was hectic," I replied.

"It had to be. Why did you return the same day? You could

have spent a few days there." He pulled down his pants and changed into shorts.

"I went there to meet him, not spend the night."

"What was the need of meeting him. Who is he to you?"

He got a scotch bottle and sat on the sofa. Without wasting time, he made a peg for himself. He reached out to the fridge again for ice cubes. He put some into his drink and looked at me. "You didn't answer me."

"I had not been able to talk to him for more than two months. That's why I had to go."

"And the guy didn't try to make contact with you during these two months?"

"No, he thought if he continued to be in touch, it would hamper my married life," I said the truth.

"The guy is right. Now, what is your problem?"

"My problem is that we were friends. And friends cannot disappear like that."

"Were you just friends?" he asked and sipped his drink.

I kept gazing at him.

"I asked you something, Meera," he said.

"We loved each other too," I responded.

"So, don't you think it is wrong to have any connection with the person you loved in the past?"

"No, I don't think so. We can still be on talking terms. I am not going to keep any kind of illicit relationship with him."

Kuldeep finished his drink in one go and slammed the glass onto the table. He poured another drink for himself.

"You are a shameless girl, Meera. How can you discuss such things with your husband? You should be thankful to me that I am allowing you to stay here in my house," he said.

"You have the right to judge me, Kuldeep. But you should also be thankful to me that I am telling you the truth."

"You didn't tell me the truth on your own. You did so only because I came to know about it."

"How did you come to know about it?" I asked.

"The daughter-in-law of the Chauhan family will go out of town in her red Mercedes, and you think I will not come to know."

"Are you spying on me, Kuldeep?"

"Not at all. I don't have time for such cheap things." He switched the TV on and changed the channels using the remote.

I went close to him and sat beside him.

"I am sorry. I should have told you about this."

"I don't have problems with you having friends, Meera. But what should I do about my family? How should I tell them that having a boyfriend even after marriage is fine?"

Honestly, I was speechless.

"I will not give a chance to complain hereafter," I said after a while.

I stood up to leave, but Kuldeep caught my hand. Our eyes met.

"When are we going to make love, Meera?" he asked.

I pursed my lips and asked myself the same question. I didn't have an answer.

Trying to release my hand, I said, "Please give me some more time."

"How much more time you want, Meera?"

"I don't know, Kuldeep."

"It looks like you're physically involved with that guy! That's why you are always satisfied."

"Shut up, Kuldeep! That's not true." I yanked my hand away from him.

"You, bloody bitch, can go all the way to Prayagraj to get fucked.

But here your own husband is asking for the past three months to touch you, and you deny him. I will show you today how hard I can fuck."

"Kuldeep, mind your language," I said in shock.

"Am I impotent that you have to go to places to get fucked?"

"You're not in your senses, Kuldeep. Let's talk tomorrow."

"Shut up, you bitch. I will get what I deserve today. I have been quite nice to you so far. But you don't deserve it," he said and lunged at me. Grabbing my hands, he threw me on the bed.

"*Kuldeep!*" I screamed. "*Stop!*"

He rolled up my saree above my knees. With his other hand, he pulled out the portion of the saree that is tucked in to keep it tight. Forcefully, he unravelled my saree. Lust was dripping from his eyes.

Next, he caught hold of my blouse and pulled it off. This set me off and I kicked his balls with all my might.

With a scream, he rolled on the bed, holding his balls.

I collected my saree, grabbed another blouse from my wardrobe, and rushed out of the room. I came out of the main door and wore the saree on the lawn. Then I started walking down the road, though I had no idea where I was headed.

[43]

Half a mile away from the house, a jagran programme was going on. A group of people was dancing and chanting kirtans and bhajans under the pandal. I went and sat at the back of the pandal. I closed my eyes and tried to forget everything. For the next twenty minutes, everything went well. The music went on playing and the devotees danced to the parody of Bollywood songs devoted to the goddess. I tried to focus on a song that was playing.

All of a sudden, the music stopped playing. And it was announced that the singer had fallen ill. The fully charged public started booing. It created quite a chaos in the crowd.

"I would request everyone to maintain peace. We all are devotees of Mata Rani. Such behaviour doesn't suit us." A voice caught my attention. A man in his late forties, wearing Mata Rani's forehead band was trying to calm the audience.

I checked my phone. There were several missed calls on my phone from Kuldeep. I switched it off.

"As you know our beloved *kirtan samrat* Vijayendra Sukla ji is not feeling well, therefore is unable to continue singing. But the jagran must go on. If anyone among you is willing to sing and lead the kirtans, I would like to welcome him or her to the stage," the same person announced on the mic.

I found this as an opportunity to heal my upset mind. Nobody from the crowd went forward. So, I decided to go. I walked all the way up to the stage and said, "I can try."

"Wow! That's great, ma'am." The person frowned, taking a closer look at me. "If I am not wrong, you are Ratan Singh Rajpoot's daughter."

I shot him a stern look and turned back. I started to walk away.

"Ma'am, ma'am... what happened?" the person stuttered.

I continued to walk. I hated that I was known in the town because of my father. Did I have no identity of my own? I heard him coming behind me.

"Ma'am, sorry, if I said something wrong."

The next moment, he crossed and faced me, stopping my way.

"ma'am," he folded his hands. "I know you are a very good singer. We need you. People need you at the moment. Please..."

I gazed at him for a while and then said, "Okay."

[44]

Three years back, a night-long jagran programme had been organised by my family during Navratris. I had sung few kirtans in that programme. I could recall one of the kirtans – *Bigdi meri bana de, o shero walli maiya.*

One of the members of the committee held a booklet in front of me, consisting of the lyrics of several kirtans and bhajans. I asked them if it had the same kirtan I had sung. He opened the page.

As I started singing, people started clapping and repeating the lines after me. It also helped me to forget what had happened with me half an hour ago.

I kept singing one bhajan after another.

I must admit that I was so deeply immersed in the kirtans that I totally forgot myself. I was put into a hypnotic trance. All I could see was the face of Mohan, smiling in front of me, showing his extra canine teeth. One after another, I don't remember how many bhajans and kirtans I sang. I didn't stop until I was jerked out of my reverie. Someone called me from behind as the bhajan I was singing ended. He was one of the committee members.

"Yes, what happened?" I asked him.

He pointed towards his right. I saw my father-in-law and brother-in-law standing there. I felt a little embarrassed and thus handed the mic to the host and got down.

"Sorry, Papa. I came away without informing anyone." I looked at him, and the next moment, turned my eyes away from him.

"Go home immediately." That's all he said.

I nodded and followed my father-in-law's instructions. I had barely walked a few steps that the host came running after me.

"ma'am!" he called out.

I stopped to look back at him.

"A mere 'thanks' would not be enough to express my gratitude towards you. Still, thanks a lot. This is my card."

He held out a visiting card to me. "We would love to collaborate with you in the future if you wish to."

"Thank you" I smiled softly.

"And you have a magical voice. My entire team has said that."

"Thanks once again."

"Thanks, ma'am. I need to get back."

"Yes, please."

And we headed to our respective destinations.

"It's very late. But we have to talk about this," my mother-in-law said when I was about to enter my room.

I stopped.

"Yes," Papa ji said. "It isn't at all normal for the *ghar ki bahu* to go out of the house at night without informing anyone. Not even her husband. And then she goes and sings bhajans and kirtans in front of the public! What's wrong with you, Meera?"

I turned to look at them. My brother-in-law, Vikram, who was three years younger to Kuldeep also stood there. We didn't speak much with each other.

"I am sorry, Papa ji. But you should talk to Kuldeep about this. Ask him why he behaved so insanely," I said in my defence.

"I have already spoken to him. Did he do anything a husband cannot do to his wife? Did he demand something he doesn't deserve?"

I lowered my head and gazed at the floor. I didn't have an answer. In a way, what my father-in-law said was right. Kuldeep was my husband. But I was in love with Mohan. In fact, I had married him first. But till when could I deny him?

"Think about this, beta. And if any problem is there, we are here to discuss it."

"Please give me some time, Papa ji. I will talk about everything," I said.

"Okay. Take your time. But let's all discuss this when you feel comfortable."

I nodded.

"Okay, you may go now," he said.

I quickly walked back to my bedroom.

Kuldeep was still drinking on the sofa. A music channel was playing songs on TV.

As he heard the door open, he glanced at me. "Oh my queen. You've come back. I thought you never would."

I went to my wardrobe and picked my night gown to wear, ignoring Kuldeep.

"Who taught you to kick a man's balls?" He commented further. "That too so hard."

I walked into the attached bathroom to change without answering him.

"Why the fuck can't you change in front of me?"

I heard his fading voice as I closed the bathroom door.

"Do you realise how painful it is when you hit one's balls? Look at these. They have doubled in size," Kuldeep kept on blabbering as I changed.

Since our wedding, I had been sleeping on the sofa while Kuldeep slept on the bed. That day, he was too drunk. I tried my best to avoid an eye contact with him. He had not forced himself on me so far, simply because I had been asking for time.

Since he had occupied the sofa, I lay on the bed.

"Has someone tied your tongue?" he asked.

"No," I gave a short reply.

"Then why don't you reply?"

"I am sleepy."

"Oh, sleepy? Where did you go, by the way? To your boyfriend? Is he in town?"

"A jagran program is going on in the nearby park. I went there," I said.

"Don't lie, sweetheart!"

I was irritated by the way Kuldeep was talking to me. I was mad about my life. It was better to die than live such a life. My only ray of hope was Mohan's selection in the UPSC. And this hope was giving me strength to bear everything.

Few minutes later, Kuldeep turned the lights off, came to the bed and lay beside me. I immediately sat up, but he caught my hand.

"No, Kuldeep, please," I pleaded.

"I have listened to you. Now, you listen to me. Keep quiet! Otherwise, you'll see the worst side of me."

My heart started beating fast due to fear, and I started showing resistance. But Kuldeep was in no mood to let me go this time. He forced himself upon me and lay on top of me. He locked my hands and kept crushing me brutally under his body until I stopped fighting. And then he did everything he wanted, hurting my soul.

After a few minutes of the push up exercise, when he finished, he rolled down to his side. That day I understood why you should never marry a person you don't love. Because neither you would be happy nor the person you got married to.

I didn't sleep that night and just kept gazing at the ceiling fan. Tears kept rolling down my cheeks from the corners of my eyes. I had lost something precious that day, and that too to a man I didn't love at all.

[45]

Few days later, I got a call from Vijayendra Shukla ji, a popular bhajan and kirtan singer in the north Indian circuit. I had replaced him when he had fallen sick that night.

"I heard your voice. It is just phenomenal. I got to know that you also won a TV singing competition few years ago," Shukla ji said.

"That's true, sir."

"Then why did you stop singing? Why didn't you try to make a career in it?"

I took a deep breath. "My circumstances didn't favour me."

"That's not the way a champion talks, Meera."

"I know, sir. But..."

"I want to work with you. I want to record an album of bhajans."

Shukla ji's offer felt like a *sanjeevani* to me. *It would be a good option to engage myself*, I thought.

While I was still lost in my thoughts, he spoke again, "If you want to take some time and discuss it with your family, I'll wait."

"No, I am ready, sir. In fact, it'll be my pleasure and honour to work with someone like you," I said.

"That is fantastic. Then let me make a schedule and get back to you."

"Okay, sir."

"But my studio is in Lucknow. Hopefully, you can come and stay for a few days for the recording."

"I will manage, sir," I said.

"Don't worry, we will arrange for your accommodation here," said Shukla ji.

"Thanks a lot, sir."

"Okay then. See you soon, Meera."

As the conversation ended, I almost jumped in joy. After a long time, there was something to look forward to.

I immediately called up Mohan and shared the news with him. He was excited as well.

"That's some news, dear," Mohan said.

"True, Mohan. Finally, I can pursue my passion after such a long break."

"Now, this calls for a party, Meera. This offer has come just four days before your birthday."

A smile spread over my lips. Mohan had remembered my birthday. "Definitely, let's have a party. I am fed up with my life. But where do we meet?"

"That's the toughest question. But please, don't come to Prayagraj."

I burst into laughter as Mohan said that.

"Okay, jokes aside, do you have any plans to come to Gorakhpur?" I asked him.

"Well, I am coming over for Diwali which is four days after your birthday."

"My family is celebrating my birthday like every year. Will you be there?"

"How can I, Meera? I don't want to spoil the whole celebration."

I understood. But without Mohan, the celebration was meaningless for me.

"At least, meet me somewhere on my birthday," I urged.

"I will try. But you know better than me how much you had to suffer after meeting me last time. Don't worry, we will chat over a video call."

"How're your preparations going?" I asked.

"They're going well. In the mock tests, I am always in the top ten in my coaching classes. I even topped one of the mock tests."

"Really, Mohan? I am so proud of you! When will your mains exam be conducted?"

"This month next year. Before that, in the month of June, prelims will be held," he said.

"This is such a long process, Mohan. You are asking me to wait for one year."

"One year and a half, to be specific."

"What!"

"Yeah. After one clears the mains, there's an interview as well."

"Oh, yeah. And when is the interview conducted?" I asked.

"Most likely in the month of February-March."

"First you tell me, you won't be there for my birthday. Now, you are expecting me to wait for a year and a half. You... just... disconnect the call, Mohan."

He laughed. "You're so sweet, Meera."

That's all he said.

[46]

My family threw a grand party on my birthday. I think they were happy with me because I had sacrificed my love for their choice. All our relatives, friends and my in-laws had gathered to celebrate my birthday. Kuldeep was happy too, needless to explain the reason. The party was organised in our large garden area.

I was dressed in a designer suit, crafted in pure georgette. There was hardly anyone in the party who didn't pay me a compliment saying that I was looking beautiful. I was happy, but was missing Mohan.

"The guests have arrived. We can cut the cake," my father said while I was enjoying a conversation with my family members.

"Of course!" seconded my mother.

Kuldeep, who stood by my side, gestured at me to proceed towards the stage. I walked on to it with my family and all the members from my in-law's side. A huge six-layer red coloured cake was placed on a black glass table. A miniature figurine of a couple stood on top of the cake.

The beautiful cake really amused me, causing a smile to form. I could literally see Mohan in that miniature, smiling at me.

"Wow, what a beautiful cake!" Almost everyone said in unison.

"Indeed. Thanks a lot, guys," I acknowledged. "Who ordered this cake by the way?"

"My sis-in-law. My sweetheart, Archana," replied Kuldeep.

I looked at him and then at my sister. I leaned to hug her.

"It looks so delicious. Now, don't make us wait any longer," Papa said, making everyone laugh.

The very next moment, the DJ played the birthday song. Everyone started singing 'Happy birthday to you...' as I cut the cake.

"I am keeping this figurine. This is so cute. Thanks once again, my little sis," I said after I had finished cutting the cake and offering small pieces to everyone in my family.

The party began and people started enjoying their drinks and snacks. Some of my college friends had also come. I was enjoying my time with them. Light instrumental music playing around the garden was soothing to the ears.

"Hey, what's going on there?" Vineet, one of my friends asked me.

I turned my head sideways in the direction he pointed. A sadhu, clad in a *bhagwa* cloth, with long hair and a beard, was trying to enter the gates to the garden. The security personnel were stopping him, but the way he reacted drew everyone's attention.

I went there and enquired. "What happened?"

"Ma'am, we have told him that a family party is going on here. But he insists on walking in," one of the security guards said.

"Jai Shri Ram!" the sadhu chanted. "I have no interest in your party. I just want to give my blessings to the person whose birthday the family is celebrating. And, in turn, I would accept some food if you offer me."

The sadhu's voice sounded familiar to me. He appeared to be honest.

"Of course! It would be our pleasure. You're welcome. Please honour us," I said. The security guards withdrew and cleared the way for the sadhu.

"Pranam, maharaj!" Papa too welcomed him with folded hands as I took him to the centre of the garden.

"*Aayushman bhav,*" he said, raising his hand.

"Whose birthday is it today?" he asked.

"It is me, Swami ji," I replied. I don't know why the sadhu was attracting my attention. As if I had known him since ages.

"Take a chair and sit beside me. On your birthday, I will teach you some good things that will help you in your life," said the sadhu.

My friends stood near me. I smiled at them. "Give me some time, guys. Till then, enjoy the drinks."

One of the helpers brought a chair and placed it beside swami ji. I sat on it.

"Simply by looking at your forehead, I can say that you're artistic in nature. Is that true?" the sadhu said.

"Yes, she is a very good singer. She has also won a TV reality singing competition," Kuldeep said, who stood with my other family members.

One of staff members came with a tray filled with dry fruits while another brought a plate of fruits. A table was placed in front of him.

"I can also say that you have a very bright future. The world will recognise your talent. What is your name, beta?"

"Meera," I replied, looking straight into his eyes.

"What a beautiful name. Meera, the greatest devotee of lord Krishna. You are her namesake."

"What else can you say about me, Swami ji?" I got curious, as he really looked enlightened.

"Give me your hand, let me see what the lines on your palm say. And, you guys, please carry on with your celebrations. Let me pour some of my knowledge onto her, and then I will leave," Swami ji said to the people surrounding us.

"And what about the food?" Ma asked.

"Don't worry. I will have it."

Everyone dispersed as I held out my hand to him. He took it in his and watched it carefully. "You're very lucky, Meera."

"This time you got it completely wrong, Swami ji."

"No, I didn't," the sadhu said.

"You did. I am not that lucky."

"Why do you feel so?"

"Because I couldn't marry the person I love," I said.

He let out a sigh. "You are lying. The lines on your palm say that you are married to the person you love."

I was shocked. How did he know such a top secret of my life?

While I was still wondering, he said again, "And if you are willing to hear, let me tell you one more important thing about you."

Now, I really got scared.

"What is that?" I asked.

"You may have two marriages in your life."

I jumped out of my skin. "Who are you?" I had goosebumps.

How could someone predict this much about someone's life? In the era of science, it was unbelievable.

What swami ji did next, made me almost jump up. He winked at me. What the hell?

Suddenly it dawned on me. Mohan? Who else could it be?

"Mohan?" I exclaimed with excitement.

"Ssshhh..." he shushed me.

Now, I could understand why I was feeling attracted towards him from the moment he had come. Those eyes were familiar.

Mohan smiled. "I wanted to surprise you."

"I am totally stumped. However, I am so glad. Can't I hug you, sweetheart?"

"You want me to get beaten up?"

"Absolutely not!" I laughed and glanced around myself to check if someone had an eye on us.

People were busy in themselves.

"I love you, Mohan," I said. He was still holding my hand.

"I love you too, Meera. I have got a gift for you."

"Really?" My happiness knew no bounds.

He got something from his bag. It was wrapped in a piece of paper. I took it excitedly and opened it. "Thanks a lot, dear."

"Wow!" I exclaimed.

It was a small statue of Radha-Krishna. "What a wonderful gift!" I was overwhelmed with emotion.

Mohan smiled. Just then, one of the servants came to me. "Ma'am, someone gave this gift for you."

It was square box. "Who gave you this?" I asked, taking it in my hands.

"Ma'am, I don't know the person. Before I could ask him anything, he disappeared."

"Okay, thanks. You may leave," I said and scanned the box from all sides to check if someone's name was there.

"What the hell!" I jumped out of my chair in shock. My hands threw the box away, but the snake that had sneaked out of the box curled up onto my hand. It had come out from the gap between the sides of the box. Its smooth skin and slithering movement made my blood run cold! I broke out into a cold sweat.

"Save me, please!" I screamed, keeping my right hand away from my body. The Radha Krishna statue was still in my fist. I grabbed it tight.

Mohan stood up anxiously. He couldn't understand what to do. Everyone ran up to me as they heard me screaming for help. Everyone wanted to help me, but seeing the snake wrapped around my body, nobody dared to come near me.

"What the hell has this sadhu done?" Kuldeep yelled out. He thought Mohan had thrown that snake at me.

"Everyone, keep quiet," Mohan said and asked everyone to move away.

I was frozen at my place. The snake moved up and curled up around my neck. I started shivering frantically.

"Don't move at all, beta."

I opened my eyes as I heard Mohan's voice. He moved closer to me carefully, without making any sound. The DJ had stopped the music. There was complete silence.

I was looking into Mohan's eyes, while Mohan's eyes were locked with those of the snake. And then Mohan swung his hand with lightning speed, gripping the head of the snake. For a moment, I felt its grip increasing on my neck. I let out a scream! Slowly the grip of the snake loosened, and Mohan pulled it away from me. I coughed and caressed my neck with my hands, still trembling.

[47]

"Who the hell sent that package?" Kuldeep asked angrily after swami ji let the snake go far away from the garden.

The servant who had handed me the packet shivered. "I don't know, sir. Before I could ask the person's name, he just sprinted away."

"This is a serious matter. Somebody tried to kill my daughter. I will not spare that person," Papa said. "Akhilesh, put your people to work to find out who is behind all this."

"Ji, Papa ji," Bhaiya said.

The servant was allowed to get back to his work. Swami ji was offered a special seat.

"Swami ji, we owe you our daughter's life. You have to accept this from us," my mother sat at the feet of the sadhu. She made me sit beside her. I knew Mohan felt uncomfortable, but he couldn't disclose his identity. Since he had saved my life, my family was in awe of him. And they decided to offer him a gold watch.

"That's my duty, Mata ji. There is no need for this," Mohan said.

"Swami ji, please, we insist," Papa said and rest of the family members seconded him.

"Look, I respect your feelings, but I am not supposed to accept such gifts from anyone," Swami ji said.

"But you have to give us a choice so that we can express our gratitude towards you," Papa said.

"I can accept only food. That is it. And I would like to have my food with Meera bitiya. Arrange a table for us."

Mohan had won my heart many times before. Once again, he did the same.

A table was quickly laid out. I sat beside Swami ji. All the other guests along with Kuldeep went to have their dinner. We were left alone. We talked and enjoyed our food. My birthday was made.

"How did you catch the snake so easily? You did it as if you have been trained," I said and tore a piece of the chapati.

"I know only one thing, that whenever you catch a snake, catch it by its head," Mohan said.

"But, Mohan, it could have bitten you. You didn't fear it at all?"

"I did. But what choice did I have? It could have bitten you," he said, putting a spoonful of rice into his mouth.

We kept looking into each other's eyes for some time, then smiled at each other.

I also shared with him one of my biggest woes – that I had slept with Kuldeep, and I hated that. I asked him if something could be done. And like always, Mohan found a way. He called Kuldeep and told him that the position of my grah-nakshatras was not going to be favourable for the next six months. He was to stay away from me. Initially, he hesitated, but then agreed.

After having dinner, Mohan left. I couldn't have asked for a better birthday gift. Diwali was a few days away, and Mohan had promised to meet me once again before leaving for Prayagraj.

Now, the question that had left everyone wondering was – who had wanted to kill me? I was a little suspicious of my mother-in-law. But someone else was surely involved as she couldn't have done it alone.

[48]

Two Months Later

Two months had passed, but we didn't get any information about the identity of the person who had sent the snake. Mohan's sadhu avatar had made sure Kuldeep keep his distance. But because of this, he started being upset with me too.

Amid all these problems, there was good news. Vijayendra Shukla sir finally invited me to Lucknow for the recording of the album he had talked about. He also made arrangements for my accommodation in a guest house in Gomti Nagar near his studio. The remuneration was settled for five lakh rupees.

That evening when Kuldeep came home, I talked to him.

"It is a matter of two weeks only."

He glanced at me sideways while unbuttoning his shirt cuffs. "Where will you stay ?"

"The company has made arrangements in Gomti Nagar near the studio."

"But how can you stay there alone? Someone from the family needs to be there."

"Why? I am not a school going kid, Kuldeep."

"If you don't intend to listen to me, why are you asking me?"

"Because I don't want to go there without your consent. And if you think it is really important for someone to stay with me, then come with me for a few days," I suggested.

"I don't have the time."

"See, you don't have time. Come for at least one day. If that is also not possible, come to drop me at least." I poured some water in a glass and offered it to him.

"When do you have to go?"

"This Friday."

"It is Monday today. Have you talked to Mummy and Papa about this?"

"Not yet. First, you have to agree. Now I will talk to them," I said.

"Let it be. I will talk to them. It would be hard for you to convince them."

I was surprised by Kuldeep's support. His behaviour had changed for sure during the past few weeks.

"Thanks a lot," I smiled hesitatingly.

"You're welcome. Can I get some coffee?" he asked.

"Of course! Let me make some for you."

[49]

One week later, the recording began in Vijayendra Shukla sir's studio. I was nervous. Even though I had been practicing since the day I had got the proposal from sir, I was not in my best form. Wearing the headphone, I stood inside the soundproof vocal booth where the singers sing. From a window, I could see Vijayendra Shukla sir, who sat with his team of instrumentalists, musicians, and sound engineers.

It took me almost the entire day to get the correct pitch and rhythm. Four to five breaks, and so many retakes were done just to record the first line of the song. But I must admit that Shukla sir was very patient with me. If somebody else was there in his place, he would have kicked me out of his studio. Anyway, finally, I got my rhythm and notes right by evening. It was a very popular bhajan – *Chalo man Ganga Jamuna teer.*

"You sang it really well. I am extremely happy with you, Meera," Vijayendra Shukla ji patted me on the back as I came out after the recording was complete.

"This would have never been possible without help from you, sir," I said.

"That credit I would take," he said and laughed loudly as the rest of the team joined him.

"It's dinner time. I am damn hungry. Hurry up, guys. Let's celebrate the successful recording," Shukla sir said.

"Where do we go, sir," Kapil, one of the team members asked.

"We will decide on the way to the parking lot."

"Okay, sir."

Soon, the team gathered again at the parking lot.

"Some people can come with me too, sir," I said as my red Mercedes was parked there.

"Take Sonu and Karthik with you. Rest of the people can come with me," Shukla sir said to me.

"Sure, sir."

"Okay, let's go to Sahib Café at Taj," Shukla sir said.

"What a place, sir!" Sonu said promptly. 'Sir is extremely happy today. Whenever he is so, he takes us to Sahib Café," he said to me.

"I am glad," I acknowledged.

He smiled at me, as my driver put the engine to life and drove the car ahead.

Seven songs were recorded for the album. It was named 'Meera's bhajans in Meera's voice'. Everything was completed within the schedule. The day I was leaving Lucknow, the entire team bade me a warm farewell. Shukla sir had also given me a cheque of five lakh rupees.

"It was wonderful working with you, Meera. I hope we can collaborate again very soon," he said.

"It is rather my pleasure, sir. Because of you, I have made a comeback. Doing what I love the most. Otherwise, I had lost all hope."

"Not to please you since you are leaving, but let me tell you that I have worked with many singers, but you have something different in your voice... something I have not experienced with anyone else."

I thought there was a reason for the same. The pain I was going through in my life had made me fragile. Emotions flow out very easily when I sang. I used to imagine Mohan as Lord Krishna when I sang, and that is why I could pour all my emotions into my singing.

With a smile, I thanked everyone and left for Gorakhpur.

[50]

As I entered my house, I saw my mother-in-law sitting with her sister and niece. I went ahead to touch their feet.

"Huh!" My mother in-law twisted her lips instead of blessing me.

However, I smiled at her sister and touched her feet as well.

"*Khush raho*!" she said.

I touched Nidhi didi's feet as well.

"That's okay, bhabhi," she said.

"I'll go change and come," I said with a smile.

"If you ask, we can make tea for you as well," my mother-in-law interrupted.

I knew she was angry with me. In fact, she was always angry with me.

"Don't embarrass me, Mummy ji. I will come quickly and make coffee for all of you," I said.

"Coffee is for VIP people like you. We ordinary people drink tea. We've anyway had it just now. So, you can go and rest. You must be very tired." My mother-in-law didn't leave any stone unturned to humiliate me.

I had nothing to say. I quietly walked into my room. However, I could clearly hear Mummy ji.

"She is the real boss of this house. She can decide what she wants and what she doesn't. She is coming back after a month. *Na jaane kaha muh kaala karwa rahi thi.* My innocent son has been trapped. If

I could, I would give her poison myself. I am sure she had been with her *aashiq* all these days," Mummy ji went on.

I tried to ignore her. But when she launched a smearing campaign against my character, I couldn't tolerate it. I came out to the living room.

"Why are you telling these people false things about me, Mummy ji? You know very well where I was," I said with a frown and turned to the aunt. "Mausi ji, everybody in this house knows that I was in Lucknow for the recording of an album. This is such great news for everyone. But instead of being proud of me, they are upset with me. And please, Mummy ji, say whatever you want, but don't assassinate my character." I folded my hands with teary eyes.

Mummy ji was stunned by my outbreak. She couldn't say anything. At the same time, my brother-in-law entered the house. And Mummy ji's temper reached another level. She told him everything and he started abusing me. I couldn't stand them and ran back into my room. I fell upon my bed and cried, remembering Mohan. The song that I had recorded as one of the songs of the album started playing in my mind.

Mere to Girdhar Gopal,
Dusro na koi...

[51]

"What should I do, Mohan? It's difficult to pass even a single day in this house."

"I can understand, Meera. But what can we do at the moment?" he said.

"I don't know. I just can't live in this house. Nobody has been able to find out who gifted me that snake on my birthday. Nobody seems to care."

"Akhilesh bhaiya was given the responsibility to find out, no?"

"Yes, but he hasn't found anything," I said.

"This is strange. What about the CCTV cameras?" Mohan asked.

"No. Not in the garden."

"Okay. Then let's do one thing."

"What?" I asked.

"It might be a possibility that the person who gave that present to the security guard might be captured in the background of some of the pictures taken by the guests," I said. "Can we explain this scenario and request them to send you pictures taken around that time?"

I thought for a while. "I'll give it a try. But how do I live in such an environment, Mohan? Please tell me."

"Please wait for one year, sweetheart."

"I may not be able to live that long under these circumstances. Also, what if you don't get through the IAS exam?" I expressed my concern.

There was no response from other side of the phone.

"Sorry, I didn't mean to hurt you or lower your confidence," I said.

"I understand, Meera. In that case also, we will marry each other. But before that, you have to get a divorce from your husband."

"That's another challenge. And it will take time as well. Let me initiate this topic with Kuldeep."

As discussed with Mohan, I created a WhatsApp group consisting of the guests invited in my birthday party. And the idea worked. In one of the pictures, one person was seen giving that gift to the security guard.

"I think I know him," I said, taking a closer look at the picture. I zoomed it to its maximum limit.

Akhilesh bhaiya, who stood by my side, looked at me. "Who is he?"

"I am trying to recall. I have seen him somewhere. But not really sure."

"You just tell me who he is. I am going to make his life hell, Meera."

His words made me happy. Most of my life, I didn't have a good bond with my brother, mainly due to the age gap, but his concern for me was a pleasant surprise.

"Yeah," I said.

By the evening, I recognised that person. I had seen him in Kuldeep's office.

Oh my god! Does that mean Kuldeep sent that snake for me? Does he want to kill me? But why? I thought to myself.

I sprinted to bhaiya's room and told him about that person.

"Are you sure?" he asked.

"Yes."

"Okay then, let me talk to Jija ji."

"No, what if he had sent him himself?"

"What! You think that can be a possibility?" Bhaiya asked, surprised.

I nodded.

"Then let me get hold of this guy myself."

"Be careful, bhaiya," I said.

Bhaiya smiled and nodded.

[52]

Two days later, Akhilesh bhaiya caught that guy and took him to his office. Initially, he didn't accept anything, but when bhaiya threatened him to hand him over to the police, he blurted out the truth.

He said Kuldeep's younger brother Vikram had asked him to do so. I wasn't shocked. Vikram was closer to his mother than Kuldeep. My mother-in-law had never liked me. So, this could have been their collective plan. My in-laws wanted to take my life. In such circumstances, it wasn't safe for me to stay there. Akhilesh bhaiya told my parents. Everyone got worried. Papa was furious at my in-laws and said that he would file a case against them for trying to kill me.

I was elated. Things seemed to be falling into place. My in-laws' side had given me an opportunity to escape my screwed-up life. Now, I had a solid point to file a divorce.

My family decided to take me back home that evening itself. But I asked them to come the next day. I wanted to talk to Kuldeep first.

"Did you find the person who tried to kill me?" I said to Kuldeep as he entered our room.

"No, we haven't found anything," he replied.

"Maybe because you're not trying hard enough."

"What happened? You look upset." He looked at me.

"Are you not concerned about the fact that somebody tried to kill me?" I asked, crossing my hands across my chest.

"Why do you feel so? I am concerned."

"If I tell you that I know the person who tried to kill me, would you believe me?"

"Why wouldn't I?" Kuldeep said. "And don't play riddles. Tell me upfront."

"Vikram bhaiya."

Kuldeep's facial expressions changed as I made the revelation.

"Have you lost your mind, Meera? How dare you..."

I knew he wouldn't believe me, and that's why I showed him that picture on my WhatsApp.

"Do you trust me now? If not, you can ask this person. He was sent by your brother. He works in your office, right?"

"I am really shocked. Why would Vikram..."

"That is for you to figure out. I am going to my parents' house tomorrow. Because they feel I am not safe here."

"What?" Kuldeep frowned at me.

"Yes. In fact, my parents were coming today itself. But I stopped them and asked to come tomorrow. Because I wanted to talk to you first," I said.

Kuldeep walked up to me. "Listen, Meera. I will talk to Vikram and Mummy also. But please, don't leave the house like this. What will people say?"

I stepped back and yelled out, "What would people say, Kuldeep? Your brother tried to kill me and you are worried about people? You aren't worried about me?"

"I am worried about you, Meera."

"No, you are not. And also, I want a divorce from you," I said and looked away from Kuldeep. This was the best time to drop this bomb also.

"Hey, that's too much, Meera. I am sorry on behalf of my family. But don't talk like that."

"I am not joking. I am serious about the divorce, Kuldeep. Our marriage is anyway a mess. You also know that I love someone else. It's not a matter of a day or two. It's about our whole life."

"Shut up! Just shut up! You should have thought of all these things before marrying me. Listen carefully, I am not giving anybody any divorce," Kuldeep said.

"Then you must defend your brother in the court," I said.

"Listen, Meera. Don't be so aggressive. And let me talk to Vikram right away," he went out of the room.

In some time, he came back with a hung face. "He is not yet home. I will talk to him tomorrow. Give me time until then."

"Okay."

Kuldeep said and went out of the room for dinner.

[53]

The next morning, Kuldeep and Vikram had a heated argument over breakfast. Vikram flatly denied the allegations and rather accused me of having a loose character. Kuldeep took my side, but nobody else did.

Around ten o'clock, my father and brother arrived. Papa talked to my father-in-law and asked for his views. He didn't accept the charges against his son Vikram, even after being shown the evidence. Rather, he said I was the culprit referring to incidents such as my visit to Prayagraj and singing in a jagran programme. He accused me of an imbalanced personality. They also hinted that I was a woman of bad character.

Finally, when no conclusion was drawn, Papa asked me what I wanted to do. I told him that I couldn't live in that house any longer since there was a threat to my life. Kuldeep tried to make amends, but when his own family was not on his side, his suggestions and arguments didn't carry much weight. Eventually, I was back to my parents' house.

At night, when we were all sitting down for dinner, the discussion began.

"What next?" Ma asked.

"Whatsoever, I will not allow anyone to kill my daughter. If you are not happy with her, ask her to improve. If she doesn't, then complain to me. But you can't just kill her," Papa continued. "We are lucky that Swami ji was present that day. Otherwise, only god knows what would have happened. They should all be behind bars."

"You are right, Papa. Looks like Swami ji arrived only to save Meera," bhaiya said.

I hid a smile.

"But we need to resolve this," Ma said.

"Yes. But until I get some sort of guarantee, I am not sending my daughter to that house," Papa said.

Ranjan bhaiya put two chapatis on Papa's plate.

"And who will give that guarantee?" Ma asked.

"I don't know. See, apart from Kuldeep, nobody is trustworthy. Instead of accepting their fault, they are accusing my daughter!" Papa tore one piece of his chapati in anger and dipped it into the dal.

"Hmm," Ma said.

"Now, if Kuldeep wants to continue his life with Meera, he has to live away from his family in a separate house," Papa announced after a while.

I was really happy that day. My family was being protective of me. The only wish I had was that they should say 'Meera, now you are free to marry Mohan'. That was wishful thinking, though. I ate my food in silence, allowing everyone else to talk about my life.

I was super happy as I spoke to Mohan at night. My room was still mine. I called him around eleven and told him about all the events that had happened during the day.

"So, what if Kuldeep agrees to live in a separate house with you?" Mohan asked.

"I should also agree, shouldn't I?" I replied.

"Hmm. So, happy now?"

"Extremely."

"So am I. Looks like god is helping us."

"Yes. Now, I am eagerly waiting for my album to get released."

"And when is that happening?"

"Vijayendra sir had said it would take a month or two," I said.

"After that you'll be a famous personality in the country. Don't forget me, Meera."

"What nonsense!"

Mohan laughed.

"You too will become the DM of a district one day. So, will you forget me, Mohan?" I asked.

"Difficult to say at this moment," he said.

"What!" I exclaimed.

He laughed again.

[54]

Two more months passed, and finally, my album was released at Hotel Taj in Lucknow on the Saavn app. A grand event was organised by team Saavn and many famous personalities attended the event. I was introduced to the media houses by Vijayendra sir. It was a great moment. My entire family was present as well. After the release of the album, people requested me to sing one of the songs from the album, and I honoured their request.

Few reporters from various newspapers talked to me after the launch. Many people took selfies with me. I felt like a star. If anything I missed at all, it was Mohan.

After the event, a grand lunch was organised by Vijayendra sir. I managed to chat with Mohan and sent him the pictures of the event. I had worn a sea green satin gown for the occasion.

You look amazing in this dress, my super star! Wish I could have been there, Mohan had replied to a picture I had sent him on WhatsApp.

Then why didn't you come?

I didn't want to create any problem.

Why would you create a problem? You could have come as a reporter this time'

Hahaha. I am always there with you. Can't you feel my presence there?'

That's an impressive line. But I would have been happier if you were present here physically, I messaged.

One day we have to be with each other physically anyway.

"Where are you lost, Meera, the superstar?"

Vijayendra sir's voice brought me back to the present. Keeping my phone aside, I smiled at him.

"Nothing, sir. Just checking my phone for any messages," I replied.

"Yes, it'll be flooded with messages. You're a celebrity after all," Vijayendra sir said.

"If at all that is true, then you are the reason behind that, sir."

"That credit I'll take," he said and laughed.

"I have something special for you, Meera. Meet me after lunch," sir said.

"Sure, sir," I said.

After lunch, Vijayendra sir told me that he wanted to sign a contract for three more albums with me. I was on cloud nine. Life seemed to be too generous towards me. He invited me to his office after a week. I promised him that I would certainly be there.

[55]

Six Months Later

"That's amazing news!" I exulted and started jumping around my room.

The UPSC CSE prelims results had just been announced, and Mohan had cleared them.

I could feel the excitement and happiness in his voice when he gave me the news. I got goosebumps.

"I knew you would do this," I added.

"Yes, Meera. I am so happy. But this is only the first step. There are two more," said an excited Mohan.

"You will get through them as well. I have full faith in you."

"You believe in me more than I myself do. Sometimes, I fear I'll fail."

"Don't. Whatsoever, nobody can separate us, Mohan. We are meant to live together."

"Absolutely! You see how things are turning out in our favour," he said.

"Yes, yes, yes. So, where are you giving me a treat?" I asked.

Mohan was in Gorakhpur for a few days.

"Wherever you say. It's your call."

"Okay." I thought for a while. "I have not gone boating in Ramgarh Taal for ages."

"So, let's go boating," he said.

"Okay, sure. And then dinner at rooftop restaurant in Raddison Blu hotel."

"Umm..."

"I know what you are thinking about. My treat!"

"But it's my treat," Mohan said.

"I will take money back from you when you become an IAS officer. Okay?"

"Okay," Mohan said and smiled.

"What is the progress on the case?" Mohan asked while we waited for our food at Raddison Blu.

"Well, Kuldeep told the judge that he doesn't want a divorce."

It'd been four months since I had filed for divorce from Kuldeep.

"And what did you say?" he asked further.

"I told the judge that I don't want to continue this marriage since there has been an attempt on my life."

A family was celebrating a birthday on the table next to us.

"So, will it be tough to get a divorce?" Mohan moved his fingers around the glass in front of him.

"No. It will take time, but eventually I should get it. I have submitted the proof in the court to support my allegations."

"And what about your family?"

"My family says that if Kuldeep is ready to live with me in a separate house, then that should resolve the issue," I said and looked into Mohan's eyes. "I don't want to explain anything to anyone now. I have seen the results of making them happy."

Mohan kept his hand over mine.

"Don't worry. I am with you."

"I know. And that is why I am relieved now."

Just then, the waiter brought our food, and we dug into it heartily.

[56]

For a few months, my life had been really good and things were looking bright. But it was short-lived. The sudden demise of my father wreaked havoc upon me. I was in Lucknow when I got the news. I was devastated. It took me several days to recover from the initial shock. Even now, I was plagued by unpleasant thoughts. Due to the nearing of his CSE mains exam, Mohan too could not give me much time, that too when I needed him the most. My recording of the next album had been postponed.

I would spend most of my days with my mother. It was a loss every family member had to cope with. But Ma was the most upset amongst us. She didn't eat for three days after Papa left us. To overcome my sorrows, I also started practicing meditation in front of Lord Krishna's idol in our home temple. On the thirteenth day ceremony of my Papa's demise, Mohan came to my house. The moment I saw him, I broke into tears. I clung to him and wept buckets. I didn't even notice that my father-in-law, brother-in-law and Kuldeep were also present. Mohan consoled me, but couldn't stop himself from breaking down too.

A shanti path was organised in the memory of Papa, followed by lunch. My father-in-law met Ma and bhaiya and took his leave. He left with my brother-in-law.

Kuldeep came to me. "So, what have you decided, Meera?"

I looked into his eyes and shook my head in denial.

"I understand everything. You won't ever be happy. That's my curse to you, bitch," he whispered to me.

I couldn't believe he said that word to me on that occasion. I had no energy to fight. I simply folded my hands and gazed at the floor as he left.

"What the hell was he saying?" Mohan asked me, coming closer.

"Nothing," I replied.

After all the guests left, I went to my room, but I realised I needed to get away. I called up Mohan and asked him to take me somewhere outside. We decided to meet in front of Gorakhnath temple.

While I was on my way to the temple, I noticed a woman waving at our car.

"Who is she?" I asked the driver.

"I don't know, didi," said the driver.

"Is she waving at us?"

"Yes, didi."

"What's the matter? Stop the car, bhaiya," I said.

The driver followed my instruction and stopped the car near that lady. I rolled down my window glass.

"What happened?" I asked her.

"Didi, I need to reach LifeCare hospital urgently. My father is admitted there, and my husband is also not in town," she said and started crying.

"Oh, okay. Get in. I will drop you there," I said. I had just lost my father. Who could understand the importance of a father in a girl's life better than me?

The woman stepped inside and sat beside me. She seeme to be in her mid-thirties.

"What happened to your father?" I asked her.

"Accident," she kept her reply short.

"Oh, I am sorry."

She didn't say a word for the next ten minutes. We were about to reach the hospital.

She opened a water bottle and drank some water from it. She held out the bottle to me.

"No, thanks." I smiled.

She took out another bottle from her carry bag. It was a small Coke bottle. She offered that to me.

"That's okay," I said.

"What okay, didi? You have helped me in my time of need. This is all I have to offer to you."

The woman made me uncomfortable.

"Please, didi. Don't refuse. I am so grateful to you! And this is absolutely new. I have not used it."

"Okay, okay. Give it to me." I took the bottle from her.

"Well, we have reached the hospital too," she said, looking out of the window.

"Yeah."

"Thank you so much, didi! I will never forget this favour in my life."

"That's okay. Take care of your father," I said.

The driver stopped the car, and the woman moved out.

I called up Mohan and told him that I would be fifteen minutes late. Then my eyes fell upon that Coke bottle that lay beside me. How affectionately she had given it to me! I picked it up and opened its cap and drank the fizzy liquid.

We reached Gorakhnath temple in twenty minutes. However, I was not feeling well. I felt dizzy and disoriented. My vision also became blurry and my heart started racing. What was happening? Everything had been fine a few minutes earlier.

Seems like Papa's loss is making me sick, I thought. But very soon the feeling became intense. I rolled over towards my left. Just then I heard someone opening the door of the car.

It was becoming difficult for me to keep my eyes open. I managed to open them slightly. It was Mohan.

"Hey, Meera. What happened?" He shook me. "Are you okay?"

I couldn't even respond, though I wanted to.

Mohan got into the car.

"Take the car to the nearest hospital," he asked the driver.

"What happened to didi?" the driver asked, worried.

"I don't know. You are driving her. You should tell me what happened," Mohan asked him. "Do you have some water?"

The driver passed him his water bottle. Mohan made me drink some water.

"I think it is because of her," the driver said.

"Who?"

"The woman didi gave a lift to," the driver said.

"Which woman?"

"I don't know. Even didi didn't know her. She gave a cold drink bottle to didi from which she drank."

"What!" Mohan exclaimed. "Quick. Drive faster."

I clutched Mohan's hand tightly. Slowly, I was losing consciousness. The voices of Mohan and the driver were fading. My eyes were closed, but I could see Mohan. I could see Mohan dressed as Lord Krishna, smiling, wearing the peacock feather, a crown on his head. And slowly that image also faded away as I fell into a deep sleep.

Mohan Speaks

[1]

I ran into the hospital corridor along with three other medical staff members. Meera lay on the stretcher, unconscious. I was soaked in sweat and my heart was filled with an unknown fear.

Meera was taken to the ICU. I was stopped at the door. In a minute, a doctor rushed into the ICU.

"Sir, sir.." I kept on calling him, but remained unheard.

In a minute, a person came out of the ICU. "Who is there with the girl?"

"It's me," I said promptly.

"Please come with me." I followed that guy. I saw Meera lying on a bed surrounded by various medical instruments and machines monitoring her vitals.

"What happened?" the doctor asked me.

"Sir, I don't know clearly, but all this happened after she drank Coke from this bottle." I gave the bottle to the doctor. "And sir, this bottle was given to her by some unknown woman."

"Okay. Let's examine this drink," the doctor said. "Anything else you want to share?"

"Nothing as such, doctor."

"Then please be outside and wait," the doctor said.

"Sir, there is nothing serious, right?" I asked.

The doctor looked at me. "Of course, this is serious. Why would she be here otherwise?"

"But she is out of danger, right?" I desperately needed some solace.

"Difficult to say anything at the moment."

"Sir, give me some confidence at least," I said.

"Sorry, young man, I don't give false hopes," he said.

I folded my hands before the doctor and said, "Please, doctor!"

He kept his right hand on my shoulder. "Please have some patience, and let us do our job. Please wait outside. And what is your relationship with her?"

I thought for a while that what introduction I should give. However, I restrained myself to her friend. "I am her friend."

"Okay. Inform her family as well, and please wait."

I came out of the ICU and waited. I didn't know how to inform Meera's family, thus asked her driver to do so. He called up Akhilesh, Meera's brother, and told him about the whole situation. Half an hour later, Akhilesh was standing opposite me outside the ICU.

Another twenty minutes passed. The doctor came out of the ICU. We immediately reached out to him. He told us that traces of poison was found in Meera's blood. Later it was found that the same poison was present in the drink as well.

The treatment was on, but the next twenty-four hours were critical.

What will happen if something happens to Meera? I wondered. *Her whole life has revolved around me. God cannot be so cruel. We were to touch the shore. We can't sink just before that.*

I didn't move from outside the ICU for the next twenty-four hours. Neither did I eat anything. I made a promise to myself that I would eat only after Meera opened her eyes.

[2]

Those hours outside the ICU felt like years. However, they finally passed. And the doctor confirmed that Meera was out of danger. I got my breath back. My eyes met with those of Akhilesh, and we exchanged a smile. I wanted to see Meera as soon as possible.

I went inside the ICU the moment the doctor allowed us. I was shocked seeing Meera's face. It had turned pale as a result of the effects of the poison. Her eyes were still closed.

I went near her and held her hand. "Meera," I called softly.

There was no movement. I called two more times. And finally, she opened her eyes.

I smiled as a few teardrops rolled down my eyes.

"How are you, Meera Singh Rajpoot?" I asked to make her feel good.

She nodded slightly in affirmation. She seemed groggy.

"Are you not going to speak today?" I asked again.

She looked confused.

"Okay, don't take much stress. Just relax. You will be fine very soon," I said.

"What's happened to me?" she managed to say.

"Nothing has happened. Just some food poisoning," I replied.

"Nobody has come to see me from my family?" she asked.

"Akhilesh has come. Archana is also outside. They will come in when I go out."

Hey wait! What kind of question that was? Why did Meera ask me about her family when I stood in front of her? Her question boggled my mind. Did she not recognise me?

"Are you not happy to see me, Meera?" I asked to get the answers to the questions arising in my mind.

She squeezed her eyes as if trying to recall something.

"I am sorry. I didn't understand. Should I be happy?" she said.

My mind was blown away. Couldn't Meera recognise me?

"Meera, who am I?" I asked, standing up at my place. Her hand slipped away from mine.

She closed her eyes. Wrinkles at her forehead clearly indicated that she was trying to recall.

"Meera, who am I?" I asked again.

She opened her eyes and smiled slightly from one corner of her lips. "I am really sorry. I am unable to recall your face or name. Could you send someone from my family, please?"

I was struck dumb.

"Meera, I am Mohan," I said a little louder.

"Oh yes, Mohan. Thanks for being here. Could you send someone from my family, please?"

She pretended to recognise me, it was clear that she hadn't.

I tried to confirm it once again. "Okay, tell me what is your sister's name."

"Who are you to ask me this question? Send my sister in and please leave me alone," she said agitatedly.

I couldn't understand what to do other than walk out of the ICU. I immediately reported Meera's strange behaviour to the doctor. He didn't believe me at first and went to get some tests done.

Surprisingly, she didn't recognise her siblings either. It was clear that Meera had lost her memory.

The doctors said that it was the effect of the poison consumed by Meera. Thankfully, she had not finished the entire bottle and had reached the hospital on time. Otherwise, chances of her survival were slim. Somehow, she had survived, but had lost her memory.

Meera's family took her to Delhi for further treatment, while I went back to Prayagraj as my CSE mains exams were nearing. It was the most difficult time for me. I couldn't focus on my studies. She had forgotten me – Meera, my strength, my motivation in life. I never expressed myself much, but for me, life had no meaning without her.

Despite the stressful situation, I tried hard to forget everything else and focus on my studies. I had to become an IAS officer for Meera. I utilised my pains and sorrows and channeled my whole energy towards the preparation.

In the meantime, Meera's family visited many famous hospitals and geriatric psychiatrists in Delhi. All the doctors suggested that there was no specific treatment for lost memory. All the people around Meera had to help her regain her memory by talking about her past, the memories of her past, the important events of her life, the good moments she spent with her loved ones, etc. They also suggested she practice yoga and meditation. Apart from that, a biweekly visit to a geriatric psychiatrist was also recommended.

Every two weeks, Akhilesh would take her to Delhi for a doctor's appointment. He would also make her talk to me on a video call. By now, he had understood my importance in Meera's life. And not only him, but Meera's whole family. Her mother also said to me several times that she herself would give Meera's hand to me once she regained her memory. Everyone was waiting for that day to come.

Meera's in-laws' family completely washed their hands off her life. That woman who took a lift in Meera's car that day was never caught.

But certain circumstances indicated Meera's in-laws' involvement in that matter. However, due to the lack of solid evidence, no immediate action could be taken against them. A case was filed against all of them. The proof of trying to kill Meera in the first attempt was also submitted in court.

[3]

In the meantime, the most awaited day of my life also arrived. The day of the mains exams and I gave my hundred percent to it.

After a few months, the results of mains exams were out and to my unbound joy, I had cleared them. Now, there was just one round to go – the interview. Celebrations were the need of the hour, but my happiness was incomplete.

After sharing the news with my parents who were elated, I went to Meera's house.

Her sister brought her to the living room where I had been waiting. She was living in her own house like a stranger as she didn't even recognise her own family members. Contrary to her personality, she looked like a timid, confused and vulnerable girl.

"Hi, Meera. How are you?" I initiated a conversation.

She looked up at me and smiled formally.

"I am good. How are you?"

"I am excellent. I have some news for you."

"What?" she asked.

"I've cleared my civil services mains exams," I exclaimed.

"Congratulations!"

The way Meera responded broke my heart. Just like a stranger.

"Meera, you remember, this is what we had been waiting for! Now, just one more step and I will be an IAS officer."

The puzzled expressions on her face said that she didn't remember anything from our past.

"I hope you get what you want," she replied.

"But, Meera, I want you." I knelt before her.

"I a... m... m sorry." She looked uncomfortable.

"Meera, I am Mohan. I am your Mohan!" I grabbed her hands which she withdrew immediately and looked away from me.

"Meera, say something. Don't be afraid," I added.

"B... but I am told that I am already married. So, how can you be mine?" she asked, still avoiding an eye contact.

"That is true. But..." I couldn't understand how and what to explain to her. I returned to the sofa.

Meera signalled to her sister to take her back to her room. I saw her turning her back on me and watched her until she disappeared from my sight.

Meanwhile, I saw Meera's grandmother coming towards the room. One of her helpers helped her sit on one of the sofa chairs.

"All this has happened because my beloved Meera was kept away from her Krishna. This family has repeated the history. What happened with Meerabai decades ago has been done again with my granddaughter," Meera's grandmother said.

Meera's mother lowered her head and massaged her temples.

"Now, only Krishna can do something good to her," Meera's grandmother added.

A song began to reach my ears and slowly its sound increased.

"Where is this song playing?" I wondered.

"In Meera's room," replied Meera's grandmother.

Main Shyam Diwani...

Mera darad na jaane koi...

Main Shyam Diwani...

Anoop Jalota ji's voice had all the pain and grief Meerabai's bhajan had in the lyrics. I had no idea where to go, but I could not stay there for sure. I stood up and walked out of the room.

*

One fine day, Akhilesh called up and informed me that there was an excellent piece of news. Meera had recalled a few things from her past. She had remembered a few events from her early past.

I almost jumped out of my skin. What could be better news for me? If somebody asked me to choose between a rank in Civil Services and reversal of Meera's memory loss, without wasting a moment, I would choose the second option.

I immediately spoke to Meera. She still didn't recognise me, but I was happy. There was some improvement at least.

Soon, the date for my interview arrived. It was time for the final strike.

[4]

Roll No. : 01xxxx7
Name: Mohan Kumar

Subjects	**Marks**
Essay (Paper-I)	144
General Studies -I (Paper II)	119
General Studies -II (Paper III)	122
General Studies -III (Paper IV)	103
General Studies -IV (Paper V)	130
Optional-I (Literature of Hindi Language) (Paper-VI)	149
Optional-II (Literature of Hindi Language) (Paper-VII)	145
WRITTEN TOTAL	912
PERSONALITY TEST	172
FINAL TOTAL	**1084**

Remarks :- RECOMMENDED

Though I was kind of confident about clearing it, seeing the result as 'RECOMMENDED' on the screen, gave me goosebumps. This was my final result on the UPSC website. I couldn't control my emotions. My eyes were filled with tears as I looked at my parents. They couldn't make out from my expressions whether I had nailed it or failed. Words failed me, and my body went numb for a few seconds. I hugged my mother tightly.

Nobody spoke for about a minute. Then my father said, "That's okay. You tried really hard." And he choked.

My mother also stroked my head. "Don't lose heart, my son."

I suddenly stood up at my place and replied with a big smile on my face, my hands on my hips. "Arrey, why are you guys behaving like I have failed the exam?"

"Meaning?" asked my parents in unison.

"Arrey, baba, I have cracked it!" I pumped my fists.

"What!"

The expressions on my parents' faces were worth watching. My father stepped forward and hugged me tight. Ma also embraced us. Both of them broke into tears of happiness.

And they started making calls to all our relatives and friends to share the happy news. The news broke out like wildfire in my entire neighbourhood. And very soon, our house was packed with my neighbours. Cracking the Civil Services exam is no less than breaking mountain rocks.

Everyone wanted to offer their congratulations, but I wanted to run away from there. I had to share the news with Meera. This is the dream both of us had been dreaming of together. I wanted to propose my love to her once again. All over again. If she didn't recognise me, then I would propose marriage to her again.

Soon, I sneaked away from my house and went to Meera's house.

[5]

"Meera, Meera..." I screamed as I entered the living room. Meera's mother walked in, but her face was tense with worry. I lunged at her feet and touched them.

"Auntie, I have cracked my Civil Services exams," I exclaimed with joy and excitement.

It was surprising to notice that there was no change in her expression.

"What happened, auntie? Is everything alright?" I asked. "Where is Meera?"

"She has been missing since the afternoon."

"What!"

"Yes. She has left her phone in her room. God knows where she has gone..." Auntie said and burst into tears.

My heart skipped a beat.

"Where are Akhilesh and Archana?" I asked.

"Everyone is looking for her." Auntie collapsed on a chair near her. "I am so worried about my daughter. Ma is right. I am responsible for her condition," she sobbed.

"Why didn't anybody inform me?" I yelled, but auntie didn't say anything. She appeared lost and in deep grief.

I rushed out of the house.

Where can she go without her phone? I wondered. A lot of things went through my mind.

Can she go to a friend? I asked myself.

No. How can she, when she doesn't remember anyone?

Then where can she go? I thought, exasperated, and kicked the ground.

I called up a friend of mine and asked him to lend me his bike. Soon, I was riding across the city lanes in the hope that I would find Meera somewhere. She must be wandering in the town itself. What would a person with a lost memory do otherwise?

In the scorching heat of May, I was looking for her in every street, road, lane of Gorakhpur city.

But even after a marathon hunt of three hours, I didn't find her. It was 6 p.m. and I had run out of petrol. I parked the bike on the side stand and sat on the pavement. Grabbing my head, I started weeping. What kind of test it was that god was putting us through?

I dragged the bike to the nearest petrol pump and got some fuel before I began my search again. Suddenly, I noticed a crowd near a park. Some kind of show was going on there. I parked my bike and went there. A group of people were playing bhajans of Lord Krishna. They looked well trained. One person was on tabla, one person was playing the dholak and one of them was on the harmonium, whereas one person was singing.

But what I saw next blew my mind away. There was Meera! Dancing to the song. And dancing as if she didn't care and as if nobody was watching her. She was in a state of complete ecstasy. She was dancing in such a way that I couldn't dare to disturb her. It would have been an insult to her and the lord Krishna as well.

I waited there for the next half an hour. Meera hadn't noticed me.

Meera stopped only after the group stopped singing and playing their instruments. She sat on the ground itself. I immediately went to her and tapped her on the shoulder, getting down on my haunches.

She looked up at me.

"What's up?" I waggled my eyebrows with a smile.

She was bathed in sweat. She smiled innocently and said, "Nothing."

I also behaved as if nothing had happened.

"Shall we go home?" I held out my hand towards her.

"Yeah."

I walked her up to my bike and rode her home. On the way, I didn't ask anything. She didn't say anything either. But I was worried. Why had she gone out like that? And why was she dancing like that? She was acting exactly like Meerabai. Had Meerabai's soul entered her body? I had many questions, but no answers.

[6]

I had told everyone at Meera's home not to react at all and to act as if nothing had happened. I sat with her in the living room. While having tea, I began to talk to her.

"Meera, would you mind if I ask you something?"

She gazed at me hesitatingly and shook her head.

"Where did you want to go? And why were you dancing in public?" I asked.

She didn't say anything for a while and kept sipping her tea.

She spoke when I asked her again, "Dadi says only Lord Krishna can bring my memories back. I trust Krishna."

"That's okay. But why did you go out without your phone?"

"I don't remember where I was going. On the way, I saw those people singing songs for Lord Krishna. I was lost listening to that magical voice that I don't remember when I started dancing. But I must tell you, I am in love with Krishna."

"Do you really not remember anything about us?"

"Sorry!" She shook her head.

I thought for a while. "Promise, you won't leave home again without informing someone."

"You care for me a lot. We must have been close."

"We were," I gazed into Meera's eyes. She turned her gaze down.

"Okay, I promise. Now, can I go to my room?" she asked.

I nodded.

After that day, Meera was frequently found dancing on the streets of Gorakhpur. Slowly, all of us understood that it was not possible to lock her inside. I discussed her situation with her doctor and he suggested that she should be allowed to do what she liked. That was probably a way to keep her normal.

I understood what the doctor suggested because I had noticed that Meera didn't dance on the street intentionally. When she did so, she was totally lost, elated, and in a state of extreme joy. Only god knew what had happened inside her head. It wouldn't be completely wrong to say that Meera was alive again on the streets of Gorakhpur city.

One evening, when I was in Meera's house, her grandmother said to all of us, "You all are unnecessarily worried about my child, Meera. She is alright."

I took a deep breath and exhaled. "You are probably right, Dadi. When she has surrendered herself completely to Krishna, there is no need to worry about her."

"What do you mean, Mohan? Should we stop caring about her?" Bhaiya asked.

"Not really, I mean that we should. We should care about her. We should make sure that she is safe wherever she goes. But we shouldn't stop her. Remember, what the doctor had said?"

Akhilesh looked unconvinced.

"Look, there is nothing much we can do." I waited for a while. "And therefore, I have decided to marry her."

All eyes in the room turned at me.

"Yes, I mean that."

"But will she agree?" asked Meera's mother.

"At least, let me try," I said.

Auntie looked at Akhilesh and then at Dadi. They approved of my proposal. Meera's husband and in-laws had not enquired about her even once. This was another reason her mother and the rest of the family didn't think twice about accepting my proposal.

"Thank you so much!" I smiled.

[7]

The next day, I took Meera to Ramgarh Taal. Who knew if she recalled everything about us there? After all, we had spent such good times at Ramgarh Taal.

I tried hard to make her comfortable with me, but she seemed distant and indifferent. I tried to make her laugh, but in vain.

Finally, I proposed marriage to her while we stood against the railing of the boating area platform. But she kept on gazing far away at the horizon. She was hardly responsive. I kept my right hand over hers, but her hand was cold.

I spent two hours with her. And eventually, I realised that it was a futile exercise to talk to her. My Meera was lost. The only option left for me was to wait. Wait till eternity.

In the evening, when I returned home, Ma sat beside me. Papa joined us as well.

"There are many proposals for you," she said.

I looked at her.

"No, I am not saying that you should marry now. First, you have to complete your training and then settle down. I'm just letting you know," Ma said.

I could understand her feelings. She was a proud mother.

I faced her. "Ma, before I say something, let me tell you that I love you, but I can't marry. And if I marry someone, then it has to be Meera."

Ma was surprised. "But how can you? She has lost her senses."

"I know what is bothering you, Ma. What will happen if she never becomes normal, right?"

"Yes. You can't spoil your whole life."

"Nobody's life gets spoiled if he chooses not to marry, Ma. And if anyone's life has actually been turned upside down, then it is none other than that of Meera. She has lost everything for me. She has sacrificed everything for me. Now, it is my turn, Ma."

"What nonsense!"

"No, Ma. That girl has become mad in my love. How can I leave her in this situation? Whatever I do for her will be nothing in comparison to what she has done for me. I will wait for her till eternity."

Ma looked at me, surprised. Papa too had come closer. He listened to our conversation, but didn't say anything.

"Yes, I can't leave Meera. In fact, I don't have to marry her, because I am already married to her. All I need is to take care of her till she gets her memory back and becomes normal."

I had tears in my eyes.

"I love both of you very much. And I love Meera too. Please don't bring up this matter again because my answer will not change," I said in a quivering voice and touched their feet before leaving the room.

"But listen to me, beta..."

Ma's words faded as I rushed out of the room.

[8]

Meera continued dancing and singing on the streets of Gorakhpur. She had become famous in the entire city, but as it happens, several stories about her started floating around. Some said she had become mad because she was ditched by her first lover, that is me. Some said it was because her in-laws caught her red-handed with her lover, and thus threw her out of the house. Some said her divorce was the reason while others said Meerabai's soul had taken over her body, and so on. The stories were endless.

Few people even hated her because they believed Meera was a girl of bad character. But most loved her because of her innocence and magical voice. A lot of people supported her out of sympathy, and various groups of devotees, especially those of Lord Krishna, started inviting her to their programmes. We deployed two bodyguards for her security, to escort her wherever she went.

Finally, the day came when I had to leave for LBSNAA (Lal Bahadur Shashtri National Academy of Administration) in Mussoorie, Uttarakhand. My training was to begin. I went to meet Meera a day before leaving. I told her about everything and that I would be back soon. For the first time, she clung to me and cried. She clutched my t-shirt so hard as if she was stopping me from going. But she didn't look at my face. Not even once.

It is as difficult to explain how I felt in those moments – akin to holding water in your fist. For a moment, I wanted to stay back. But then I realised that this was Meera's dream more than mine. She didn't utter a word, but just kept standing, holding me and hiding her face in my chest. Her sobbing was heart-wrenching. I too wept along with her.

Around ten minutes later, finally, she spoke. "Please, come back soon," she sobbed.

I couldn't reply to her and just caressed her back. After few seconds, I consoled her, "Don't worry, I will be back very soon. You just take care of yourself."

I took her hands in mine. She stepped back, still gazing at the floor.

"Okay, Meera? Eat your food on time. Wherever you go out, go with your bodyguards, and inform someone in the family. And always keep your phone with you," I said. "I will keep calling you."

She sniffled.

I drew my hands back as I was about to leave, Meera's hands slipped slowly over mine. Her fingers seemed to be reluctant to let my hand go. But eventually, our hands separated. I rushed out of the room without looking at Meera. Because if I did so, I wouldn't have been able to leave her.

Those moments were painful. I felt as if someone had ripped out my heart.

[9]

"Coming up next is a beautiful devotional song in Anup Jalota ji's voice. I personally love this song very much. Truly said, if you love someone, love like the great Meerabai - with complete devotion, and complete surrender to your lover. And what can be better if it is god himself!" a female RJ said on BIG FM.

I had just got into my cab taking me to the railway station. It was early morning.

The RJ continued, "Let's fall in love with Lord Krishna. Guys, you know Lord Krishna has several names - Govind, Kanhaiya, Shyam to name a few. So, this song is dedicated to Krishna by Meera. So, here comes the beautiful song for you."

Aisi laagi lagan, Mira hogayi magan
Woh to gali gali hari gun gane lagi
Mahalon me pali, banake jogan chali
Mira rani diwani kahaane lagi...
Rana ne vish diya, maano amrit piya
Mira sagar me sarita samaane lagi
Dukh laakhon sahe, muh se Govinda kahe
Mira Govind Gopal gaane lagi

Tears continued to stream down from my eyes as I closed them and remembered Krishna.

"Please take care of my Meera," I said. I was happy because I believed that Lord Krishna would take the best care of Meera.

"Here it is," said the driver and stopped the cab. I paid him and walked towards Gorakhpur Junction.

*